Enjoy!

Saúl
Coullard

In loving memory of those who have passed before us.

A.D.C.

C.K.L.

D.J.L.

Author's Note:

In this book you will come across some terms which may otherwise be unknown to anyone outside of the Upper Peninsula of Michigan. Let us have a quick lesson.

U.P.

Upper Peninsula of Michigan, home of The Yoopers. Chosen race of The Bullhead Gods.

Yooper

Anyone who was born and raised in the upper peninsula of Michigan. Well known for their skills in hunting and fishing. They are also well known for their love of strong alcoholic beverages, gambling and maple syrup. Tend to overuse 'eh' in their statements.

Troll

Anyone who lives below 'the bridge' (Mackinac Bridge) which connects the Lower and Upper Peninsulas. Well known for traveling up north to shoot deer with rifles because most of the Lower Peninsula only lets them use shotguns. They also seem to think 'Northern Michigan' means the areas of Petoskey or Rogers City.

Eh

A word commonly overused by Yoopers to end statements, eh. Contrary to popular belief, the word 'eh' was invented in The Upper Peninsula and not in Canada. They just stole it from us because they are dicks like that. Canadians say 'eh' after a question and Yoopers say 'eh' after a statement. Example:

Canadian – "What are you doing eh?"

Yooper – "Drinking a beer eh."

Intro

Most people have a good recollection of their first childhood memory. Whether it's a memory of their first Christmas, birthday, receiving a new toy or a special time with their relatives, they have a good idea which is their first.

I really only have one memory that sticks out in my mind as being the first and I was around two years old when this memory occurred. I remember standing in the garage with my hands raised towards the ceiling, crying and reaching for a gas can. The gas can I was trying to reach was hung from the ceiling by way of my parents who recognized that I had a problem. My problem was that I was addicted to huffing gas. I would sneak into the garage while my parents weren't looking to hop on a gas can and snort the fumes until I would pass out. My mother recalls a few times where she had to give me cold baths and walk around outside with me in her arms trying to get fresh air into my lungs due to poisoning myself. After the first three times she didn't even bother to call poison control anymore. Hell, I even remember talking to people who would just appear out of thin air while I was high! I remember this one guy in particular who was about 3ft tall, glowed green and was smoking a pipe. He was a spitting image of Lucky, the cereal leprechaun. I'm not too entirely sure what all we talked about as one minute he was standing before me and the next I would be flat on my back moaning & unable to get up. I always remember that after having a good session of huffing gas I would always giggle aloud because I could see myself in a third person view, staggering wherever I walked. I never could hide the smell of gas from my parents though nor could I hide my barbaric nature of speaking in grunts and not being completely coherent. Needless to say, I spent a lot of time flat on my back before my parents realized that I had an actual drug problem and wasn't just semi-retarded. It wasn't long after that they started to hang all the gas cans from the ceiling so I wouldn't get into them. This was also a start to a life that would be anything but normal. When one's first memories are that of huffing gas, you can only imagine what the future will hold for that individual eh.

Holy Exploding Lawnmowers!

It was around my freshman year in high school when two buddies and I decided to skip class. Billdo, Dentis and I decided that it was too nice of a day and we needed to go do something other than learning.

Billdo and Dentis were two of my best friends. Dentis was the oldest of us and was usually the one who called the shots. Eager for mischief and never able to sit still, Dentis was usually in trouble (in school and at home) and was always itching for more action. Right or wrong, he was always on the go with not a moment to lose. Billdo was the shadow of Dentis. Usually together, Billdo always did whatever Dentis would say. Billdo also had an unnatural attraction to alcohol and was never afraid to get falling down drunk by 9am. I was the youngest by two years but that never seemed to make a difference. Together, the three of us were always causing trouble and ready for the next big thing.

As soon as the bus hit the school, we marched downtown and took a back woods trail to the river which wasn't far off from Billdo's house. We stayed at the river for a couple of hours clubbing suckers (fish) because we had to wait for Billdo's parents to leave the house. As soon as we knew they were gone, we made the jaunt to his house. Once we got there, we opened up the gun cabinet and armed ourselves with a couple 12 gauges, a .22 long rifle and an old .303 British. After we had plenty of ammunition and a healthy stock of Billdo's Dad's beer, Billdo busted out their brand new lawn mower for some extra entertainment. Seeing that the grass was long, he decided to mow some of it by cutting a big pattern of a cock and balls right in the front yard. You could definitely tell what it was due to the sheer size of it. Once this was complete, Billdo then decided we needed a jump for the mower. Dentis and I said that it was a stupid idea because it only went 5mph for top speed. While Billdo was riding around looking for a jump, I shot his only basketball, a humming bird with the humming bird feeder and Dentis shot a shit covered duck in the cesspool out back. Billdo had finally found a neat little mound to jump his mower off of. He was going wide open (5mph) at the mound and as soon as he hit, the mower deck caught on a root. It was got yanked back just enough to get caught under the tires and was ripped completely off by the spinning back tires.

We laughed like hell at Billdo's dumbass move for

about an hour straight. He was really bummed because he had no idea how he was going to explain this to his parents. The mower being brand new and all, we knew that his ass was going to be in trouble when his parents got home. Dentis then decided that he was going to ride around on the mower for a little bit before Billdo put it away. I was sitting on the porch with a 12 gauge and the .303 brit in my hands just waiting for some kind of creature to come by when Dentis first took off. He drove into the yard and tried going up a little incline but the tires started spinning which brought him to a stop.

Enter Billdo.

Billdo seen that the tires were spinning so he got a bright idea to jump on the back of the mower so it would get enough traction for Dentis to take off. That mower got some traction alright. As soon as Billdo jumped on, it flipped over backwards (still running) and sent both of them flying away from the mower.

It was like a scene from die hard. They both got up off the ground and started running when suddenly, a mushroom cloud of fire and black smoke exploded right behind them. Apparently when the mower flipped over on its back, it busted the gas tank somehow and managed to turn itself into a 500lb bomb. The mushroom cloud went about 50ft in the air, was about 20ft wide and the whole immediate area around the mower was covered in flames. We all stood there speechless for a few minutes trying to figure out what the hell had just happened. Dentis finally broke the silence: "Man… and you thought you had some explaining to do about the mower deck." Dentis and I laughed until we cried while

Billdo just flat out cried. "My parents are going to kill me!!" he kept saying over and over. We finally got the hose and put out the lawn mower and other parts of the yard that were still on fire. Once we had it all put out, we took a look at the mower to see how bad it was.

The explosion was so powerful that it blew all the motor mounts off the engine, melted a hole through a tire, melted the gas tank (which was on the back of the mower) damn near into a plastic ball, all the wires melted and everything that was plastic on it was burned off. We put it together the best we could, pushed it into the garage and covered it up with a bunch of various items so it wasn't so visibly noticeable. Once we had it decently hidden, we sat on the deck with the guns trying to come up with a plan for poor Billdo. While we were sitting there discussing various options, Billdo raised the .303 british, took careful aim at a stop sign that was about 250 yards away and shot. Instead of hitting the stop sign, the bullet went about another 150 yards past it and hit a cow. We heard a loud "whack" when the bullet struck then we heard a sickly "mooooo" from the cow. The big animal then went down to one of its front knees….then another knee…and another… and then it just fell over.

We ran inside, threw the guns into the cabinet, hid all the ammo and ran through the woods back to school as fast as we possibly could.

Billdo had gotten home just in time that night to get yelled at for the giant cock in the yard. Next, his dad opened up the garage and started walking towards the mower while still cussing out Billdo for being a "dumb asshole". As soon as he lifted the canvas we had placed over it, he jumped back and gasped.

Billdo then asked his father in a loud, astonished voice… "What did you do to it Dad!?"

Thou shall not drink and drive eh.

I was around 17 years old and was out driving around in my little Dodge Dakota (The Red Baron) one day when I decided: "You know what? I'm going to have a party!" I made the calls and before I knew it, there were about 40 people at my cabin all ready to party it up. The party went really from what I can recall. People were shooting at the moon with guns, someone set the road on fire and someone even nearly drowned in the ditch that night. It was a good time and there were no deaths or dismemberments despite the shenanigans that were taking place. I remember standing around drinking beers with all my good friends when suddenly, everything went black. The next thing I know, I was picking myself up off the ground next to the fire and everyone else was gone! I wasn't too sure where everyone went in such a big damn hurry but low and behold, they were all gone. The only thing I could think of at that moment was my nice cozy bed that was waiting for me at home. So I hopped into my truck, turned the key and once again blacked out.

I woke up lying in the drive way of my parent's house with my mom kicking me in the ribs shouting "Get up!!! GET UP!!! Get into that house and go to sleep right now!!! Ugh! No way I'm taking you to church this morning!" I started to look around so I could get a grasp on what the hell was going on when a couple things out of the ordinary caught my attention. My truck was still running, in gear and was completely buried up to the axel in the yard with the nose of it pressing up against the house. The camper, which was sitting in the driveway, was blown off the jack stands and had somehow rolled out into the yard. There was a mailbox that had magically appeared in the driveway as well. Judging from the scene of the crime, it was hit by a vehicle at high speeds because the 10in cedar post was snapped like a twig and it had a big mark where a bumper had hit it just above the break. Who would do such a thing?

Apparently, the mailbox which was jammed into my grill somehow fell off when I pulled into the driveway. The bumper on my truck was the same exact height as the tongue of the camper so when I failed to stop, it was knocked off the jacks and rolled out into the yard. Once again, by looking at the evidence of the current situation I was in, a couple other things were determined. After the camper was knocked into the yard, I must have opened another beer and tried to rectify my driving miscalculation but only made it as far as opening the door of my truck. Once the door was opened, I fell out onto the gravel and passed out with the full beer still in hand. My truck (which was still in gear) idled further into the driveway and finally made it far enough through the yard to hit the side of the house. After the truck made contact, it just sat there for about 4 hours and slowly spun the tires on the wet grass until it was buried up to the axel.

As my mom was yelling at me to get into the house, other relatives (grandparents, aunts and uncles, cousins…) were all driving by and heading off to church. They of course had to stop, stare and laugh for a little bit before they headed out which made my mother that much angrier with me. I started to walk into the house when my father met me at the door. "We're going to church. I want everything back the way it was by the time I come back else it's your ass. Oh, and… I'm just oozing with pride right now, son." He said sarcastically as he strutted out the door to the car.

…to this day, I still don't know where that mailbox came from.

The plight of the Jehovah recruiter

It was a Saturday morning a number of years ago. The sun was warm, the beer was cold and my brother and I were just sitting around enjoying the weather.

My brother is about ten years older than me and was always my idol growing up. Never afraid to drink one too many beers or dive head first into a dangerous situation, he always had my full admiration. Seeing as though I was the younger one, I always had to do whatever he told me to which usually involved something illegal or life threatening.

Just as we were discussing what we should do for the day, a skunk ran across the yard. The nerve of that dirty little bastard! How dare he run across my brother's yard! Apparently he wasn't able to read the sign that said "Trespassing on this Yooper's property is punishable by death."

As the skunk was running across the yard, my brother and I ran into his house to arm ourselves. He grabbed his 9mm pistol with 2 full clips and I grabbed a 12 gauge along with a handful of shells. We knew the skunk was on the move and that time was getting short so we rushed to the door with our guns loaded and ready. My brother opened the door abruptly and it came to a sudden stop as if something was blocking its path. "What the hell? Move you miserable bastard!" He yelled. Thinking that his dog was in the way of the door, he put his shoulder down and bull rushed it with all of his weight. "I swear I'll shoot you yet you dumb son…" and he suddenly stopped talking.

To both of our surprises, there was a man in a suit laying flat on his back and a pile of pamphlets were scattered about him on the muddy ground. My brother and I were standing above him, both wielding guns as if we were ready to storm a beach. Still full of adrenaline and amped up to kill the skunk, my brother spoke without thinking. "Holy shit! I thought you were my dog and almost shot through the front door!" The man's eyes darted back and forth between my brother and I as he franticly started spitting and sputtering out his explanation. "M..m..m...m..my....my name is....uhhhhh... I'm from the witnesses of Jehovah." As he was talking, he was slowly getting up with his arms raised as if he was being held hostage. "I... I... I'm handing out pamphlets... a..an...an...and there's yours!" he said as he pointed to the ground. As soon as my brother and I both looked at the ground, the man turned around and sprinted to his vehicle. He got into the car, threw it in gear, spun out in the driveway and started to drive off. As he was flying out of the driveway, the skunk came running out of the ditch just in time to get ran over. The animal blew apart in a green mist of skunk spray which engulfed the man's car but he didn't even hit his breaks. That man was getting the hell out of there and he wasn't looking back.

"Huh. I'll be damned." My brother said as he stood there looking down at the pamphlets.
"I definitely didn't expect that…" I said still watching green mist of skunk spray settle in the driveway.
"You think he'll ever come back?" my brother asked.

"Nah, I don't think so. I'm pretty sure he now knows we're Catholic." I replied with a grin.

The fourth annual bullhead derby.

Let me start off by explaining what a bullhead is exactly. A bullhead is nothing more than a smaller version of a catfish and is usually .5 – 2lbs in weight. Every year, a bunch of us Yoopers would rally together in mid July at the local camp ground and have a derby. There were no prizes of any kind in this derby except for bragging rights. Even then, you can only brag so much about catching the most bullheads. Size didn't really matter unless it was really, really small. These young ones got tossed back with hopes that they'd grow into a wall mounter some day. If all else failed and your luck was really, really bad, you would have to make a sacrifice to the Bullhead Gods. Some of us believe that the Bullhead Gods are the overseers of extremely drunk, carhart and flannel clad Yoopers who pass out and wake up smelling like booze and decay.

They are vengeful spirits and often hold no room for the weak or well mannered. Needless to say, they're good folks to have on your side eh.

That year, we had quite a good crowd of people who were eager to participate in the derby and claim the bragging rights all to their own. My brother happened to be the camp ground supervisor also which meant we could damn near do whatever we wanted. Out of town people felt awfully nervous when they came up to the supervisor's camping spot only to see 60+ people yelling, drinking and carrying on in front of a 20ft tall fire. The derby wasn't starting until 10pm that night as the best bullhead fishing takes place after dark. Six hours later of drinking and getting our game faces on, we decided it was time to launch our campaign against the bullheads.

There were around 15 boats of all sizes (none of which had running lights) and about 60 people in attendance. I was Captain of my own vessel (a 14^{ft} aluminum skiff with a 15hp Mariner) and had a crew of three including myself. My crew consisted of none other than the thick headed Pollock, Fatious Maximus and the previous year's derby winner, Jut.

Fatious was another one of our derelict friends who was usually with us for most of the wild rides. Being 100% Polish, he was never one for quick thinking or intelligence. With his retard strength and ability to out drink (and out eat) most human beings, he was a perfect fit for a crew member. Jut on the other hand was older than all of us by a few years. This does not mean he was any wiser than any of us however. Despite this fact, he was usually the one we all went to for advice in almost all matters as he always had crude and unusual ways of dealing with all things. Jut would have made the perfect captain if he owned his own boat but because of this dilemma; he was forced to sign on with my vessel and I.

We had three thirty packs of beer with us and were each equipped with an ugly stick fishing pole. For a tackle box, we had an empty 12 pack container full of random jig heads along with a one gallon bucket full of night crawlers. Bullheads don't have much imagination when it comes to food and will bite on anything you put in front of them so we were more than ready for the evening.

The time finally came for everyone to man their boats and head out the river to the glorified bullhead hole. I can only imagine what the other campers were thinking when they seen 60 some people go staggering to the river carrying multiple coolers full of beer. People were shouting left and right, as loud as they could;

"I STUBBED MY DAMN TOE ON THE DOCK!" yelled one guy.

"DON'T FORGET THAT BOTTLE OF JACK DANIELS, WOMAN!" yelled another.

"I'LL BURN THIS GODDAMN PLACE DOWN IF SOMEONE DOESN'T GIVE ME A BEER!"

"MY FISHING POLE JUST FUCKING SNAPPED IN HALF!!!"

"GRAB THE COOLER!"

"GO FIST YOURSELF!!!"

"SOMEONE GRAB THAT MASTER BAIT!!"

Among all the yelling, there were sounds of beer bottles clinking together, people falling into the river and the roar of multiple boat motors being started. The crew and I were one of the first boats to hit the open river and start making our way up to the mouth. As we all went full throttle through the 'no wake' zone in the park, people were throwing beer cans onto the bank at the other campers.

"TEN CENTS FOR YOUR KID'S COLLEGE FUND!" yelled someone from the boat behind us. "WE'RE NOT LITTERING!!! WE'RE DONATING TO THE ALUMINUM DIKE FOUNDATION!" screamed another from the same boat. Jut yelled "BOW DOWN TO THE BULLHEAD GODS YOU HEATHENS!" to a group of natives who were also camping. It was quite the spectacle to behold if you were anywhere near the river I was told. It's not every day that one gets to witness a horde of drunken Yoopers break every moral and manmade law ever conceived from their camping site with their kids.

Once our circus of misfits and drunks managed to get through the park and up to the mouth of the river, the 4th annual bullhead derby was in full swing. The night was illuminated by a full moon and countless stars in the sky which made it the perfect night to catch some bullheads. I was just starting to get a bite on my pole when all of the sudden, a pair of arms wrapped around me from behind and drug me right into the river! My brother stripped down to his boxers and managed to swim silently over to my boat and yanked me from my seat.

"FOUL!!!" yelled Jut who was mad that our fishing hole had been compromised.

"Got'em!" yelled my brother as he dove under water back towards his pontoon boat.

"This means war!" I yelled as I stood up (the water was 3.5ft deep) and hopped back into the boat. "Fatious! Hit those bastards with everything we got!"

"Sure thing!" said Fatious as he chugged his

freshly opened beer. We used everything available in the boat for ammunition which included ice cubes, split shot sinkers, empty beer cans full of water and even two of our precious bullheads. "DIRECT HIT!" yelled Fatious as one of the bullheads struck true.

***Authors note*️**

It should be mentioned that bullheads (just like catfish) have spines on them. One is located on their back and the other two are located on either side for a total of three razor sharp daggers. Mixed with the toxins of fish slime, this makes for one painful puncture wound.

"I'm HIT!" yelled one of my brother's crew mates. "IT'S STUCK IN MY BACK!! GET IT OUT! GET IT OUT!!! GET IT OUT!!! I'M BLEEDING TO DEATH!! GET IT OUT!!"

"Should I grab the oar and knock him out?" I heard another crew member ask. "Just grab it and rip it out of his back!" yelled my brother. "And quit screaming like a little girl! It's just a little bullhead you big pansy!"

"It stings!! At least kill it so it will stop flipping from side to side!!! It's tearing a hole in my back!" said the man in a whiney, pathetic voice. Before anyone could reach the wounded man, the bullhead managed to flip and wiggle out of the man's back on its own.

"Holy shit that hurts!! HEY! PHILLIP!! Next time, do me a favor and just use a rifle! That'll be way more humane!" yelled the man across the river. Jut, Fatious and I laughed like hell for at least five minutes. Once the dust settled and everything was seemingly calm, the fish started biting again. One after another bullheads were being hauled out of the river and into our buckets. Over a time frame over 60 minutes, my boat managed to haul up 20+ bullheads.

Everyone was catching fish all around us but it seemed like the crew and I were in the best spot as we were catching them more consistently than everyone else. As the alcohol started to fully take over my brother, he began to get jealous of my boat and decided that enough was enough.

The old 40hp Johnson on the pontoon boat fired up, creating a thick black cloud of smoke which engulfed the light of the sky.

"RAMMING SPEED!" yelled my brother to his crew. "TAKE NO PRISONERS!"

They didn't even bother to take out the wooden poles that the boat was tied to. My brother just shoved it into gear and gave it full throttle.

Luckily for us, we weren't tied to anything and we had a way lighter boat with a small crew. With one quick tug on the pull rope, the motor fired up and we were on full step within 5 seconds. "DAMN YOU!!!" I heard my brother yell as we took off. It was the perfect get away up until I jack knifed my friend's boat about 10 seconds into the trip. We hit the other boat just hard enough that Jut went flying over the bow and into their boat.

"QUICK JUT! GRAB THEIR COOLER AND GET BACK IN HERE!!" I yelled as Jut flailed around on the floor. Luck sure was on our side because before they were able to recover from the initial impact of the collision, Jut did just that. With a quick shove off from their boat and a leap of faith, Jut made it back into our boat with their cooler and a tackle box. "We struck riches Captain!" said Jut laughing. "

"ARRGGGG!" exclaimed Fatious as loud as he could while trying his best to imitate a pirate. "There's no stopping us now!" I said to them as I gave the motor full throttle and shot water all over the other boat.

For some reason, everyone else in the derby figured it was over when they seen the pontoon boat and my own little skiff driving around on the river. Everyone seemed to pull up their lines and likewise fire up their motors at the same time. My crew and I raced way ahead of everyone else only to double back into a little fork in the river which was out of sight from everyone heading back towards the park. We sat there for a few minutes waiting for our target, the pontoon boat, to pass us up so we could take them from the rear and try to hijack it. As we sat there with the motor off, we readied our supplies of various materials to throw at them and quickly slammed down another beer. A few minutes later, our target drove by at a very slow rate of speed. Due to the fact that there were about a dozen people on the pontoon, their speed was severely crippled.

We waited until the pontoon boat got about a hundred yards ahead of us then I fired up the motor to give chase. "Ramming speed!" I yelled to Jut & Fatious as we sped towards the boat. No one even noticed we were coming from behind until the very last minute when we rammed the rear of the pontoon. We managed to take out their throttle cable which would had left them crippled if it weren't for my brother... he saw the problem right away and jumped on top of the motor, manually pulling the throttle cable from the motor with his hand. Someone else took control of the steering wheel and between their quick actions, the boat didn't slow down nor was it crippled.

 Just as I was pulling along side of the pontoon

boat with Fatious ready to jump aboard, the damnedest thing happened. Right before Fatious was going to jump, one of my brother's crew members, Dan, leapt into action with hands full of some unknown substance. He managed to throw one hand full (which completely missed us) but got lost in his momentum, hit the guard rails on the side of the pontoon and fell overboard. I had to swerve hard to miss Dan and damn near threw Fatious out of the boat as well. I stayed neck in neck with the pontoon, waiting to see if my brother was going to go back and rescue his crew member. "Fuck'em! Leave'em behind!! We're going faster without'em!!" he yelled as they kept on going down the river.

Seeing an opportunity to boost my own crew by one, I made a u-turn and went back to get Dan. "Welcome aboard! You can take your post at the bow of the boat eh. Grab a beer and some ice to throw because you're now property of this boat and her captain!" I said to Dan, simultaneously throwing him a beer while opening another for myself. "Aye Aye Captain!" Dan said enthusiastically, "I'll grab…..some beer….whickey… hic…fish… hic…"

"Aw shit… Dan's wasted!" said Jut as he pointed and laughed at Dan.

"We should just throw'em back overboard! He's slowing us down and he's entirely useless!! He can't even stand and he's a stupid troll none the less!!!!" Fatious said, likewise laughing.

"Well shit… I didn't plan on this at all…" I was thinking to myself. With Jut and Fatious in the middle seat and Dan up front, our speed was cut down by half. We were barely even able to catch up with the pontoon boat and once I did, I stayed on the other side of the river to avoid attention. They were all laughing, yelling and throwing beer cans... way too busy to notice us slip past them on the other side of the river. I was planning on going ahead some and then doubling back to take the pontoon boat head on but we ran into complications.

Upon deciding that I was going to make a hard left turn and go straight at the pontoon, another boat caught my attention. Off in the distance, coming straight at us was Dentis's boat and he had a crew of about 8 people in it. His boat had a 10 more hp on mine and it was a 16ft instead of a 14ft. As he came straight at us, I recognized the boat and quickly took it for an ally. Figuring that Dentis wouldn't do anything to jeopardize my current mission, I decided just to wait for him to pass us by so I could then take my hard left turn. Just as Dentis passed us, the first wave of his wake hit the side of my boat which threw Dan (who was standing at the very bow of the boat) off his balance. Upon losing his balance, Dan fell over. This wasn't just a little accident where any person falls over, this was a 250lb man who was completely wasted falling over and not even attempting to catch himself. As he fell over, the sudden weight shift in the boat brought the front right of the boat just low enough so the second oncoming wave from Dentis's boat over took the bow. Within the blink of an eye, my boat was completely gone and all that was left were a floating cooler, a gas tank, three Yoopers and a damn troll.

Dan the troll didn't even bother to see if anyone was ok… he just swam to shore and ran off into the woods without saying a word. As for Jut, Fatious and I, we were desperately trying to grab the cooler but decided to leave it when we heard my brother yelling at us from behind: "RAM'EM!

RUN'EM DOWN!!! DESERTERS! THE WHOLE DAMN LOT! RUN'EM DOOOWWWNNNNN!!!!!!"

We all swam to shore and laid in the mud, trying to catch our breath and figure out what the hell just happened. My brother and his crew snatched up our cooler and kept driving by with someone yelling "Can't win the derby without your boat and yer fish eh!"

"SHIT!!! The BULLHEADS!!" Jut yelled as he slammed his fist into the mud.

"To hell with the the fish! They just ganked our cooler!" Fatious said while pointing at the pontoon boat.

"To hell with the fish AND that cooler! My goddamn boat is gone!!!" I yelled at what was left of my crew. We all started laughing and decided to come to a temporary cease fire agreement with the rest of the fleet so we could all work together to recover my boat.

About 15 minutes into multiple people diving underwater to tie a rope onto the boat somehow, someone from the pontoon boat yelled "Hey! Isn't that Dan's bike?"

Dan had apparently ran all the way back to camp to grab his dirt bike to "provide light" which he told us later in the night. A few of us were looking through the woods onto the dirt road, watching his headlight come bouncing towards us when we heard a loud "CRACK" and the headlight disappeared. About the same time this happened, someone came up from the water yelling "I did it!" which meant the rope was tied onto the boat. Forgetting about Dan and his dirt bike, the lot of us pulled on the rope and brought my boat to the surface. Once the boat was up, we drug it to shore and bailed it out the rest of the way so it could float. The boat was ok and my brother promised that we could get the motor running again in the morning as "this kind of stuff happens all the time". We loaded back up in the boat and got towed into camp by the pontoon boat and its crew. As we were slowing going down the river, people were yelling at us from the camp ground side saying that we were being too loud and waking up kids.

"BITCH! Most of us LIVE here!! If you want to make it through the night, I suggest you just mind your own damn business and DO NOT PISS OFF THE LOCALS!" yelled someone from the pontoon boat. I would have guessed my brother yelled it but, he didn't. "Where is my brother anyways?" I was thinking. Just as I thought the question, I immediately had an answer. He was sitting on the boat motor slumped over with a beer in his left hand while holding the throttle cable in his right... he was passed out.

A little time went by and we made it back to the boat launch with no other causalities. Most everyone just left their boats on the shore line as everyone was way too drunk up to try and load them onto trailers. We woke up everyone who was passed out in various boats (including my brother) and made our way back to camp. Due to everyone being so drunk and talking about the crazy ride back in, no winner of the derby was officially announced. We were all standing around drinking and laughing when someone piped up from the back and asked "Where's Dan?"

"Oh shit! Dan! We forgot all about him!!" I said after I got done choking on my beer "I think he hit a tree or something with his bike!!!" No sooner the words left my mouth, a voice from behind agreed with me by saying: "Yup. I sure did." Dan came walking into camp, dragging his dirt bike by the front tire which was severely mangled. Apparently, when we first sank the boat, the first thought he had was to find some light so everyone could see. Never mind the fact that 3 other people were in the water and there was potential that none of them could swim… we need some light to see what the hell just happened! He ran back to camp, grabbed his bike and hauled ass back to the spot where he figured we still were. As he was approaching our location, he noticed all the shadows on the river so he tried to show off by doing a trick on his bike. It would have been a lot cooler if he hadn't of cat walked his bike directly into a big spruce tree at a high rate of speed. The front tire and all the plastics were busted on the bike and his face was torn up pretty good as well. He had a fat lip, black eye, scrapes and scratches all down his body and the world's biggest smile on his face. "That shit was AWESOME!! Tell me someone seen it!?!?"

"We seen a headlight… heard a crash and watched the headlight disappear…other than that, nope. We didn't see it." Jut replied.

"Shit! That sucks man… that really sucks!"

About the same time Dan realized that no one even saw his spectacular motor bike crash, a group of people started laughing uncontrollably in the next camping site over. Wondering what all the commotion was about, Dan and I staggered over to see what the big deal was. Standing in the middle of 12 or so people in a circle was one of my buddies chewing the head off of a bullhead. It was his first ever bullhead that he caught and everyone made him believe that this is a ritual to chew your first catch's head off. After a couple minutes of chewing, biting and tugging, he turned around and spit the head into another man's face. Laughing even harder, the group of people couldn't believe he had just done that. "It's not too bad man… kind of chewy but not bad!"

The man then proceeded to grab a fishing pole, let some line out and began to floss his teeth. Due to being entirely too drunk, he tripped over a root while flossing and fell to the ground. He did a half assed pushup to get himself up off the ground then turned around to look at us with a very surprised look on his face. The jig head which was on the fishing pole he was using to floss had gone through his upper and bottom lips, piercing them together. The crowd damn near fell over from laughter this time. Even Dan who was still bleeding from his face laughed until he damn near passed out from pain. "From here on out, that man's name is bubblehead!" Dan said through teary eyes and laugher.

Luckily for bubblehead, we had a pair of wire cutters laying around so all we had to do was clip the hook's barb and yank it back out. "Hope you're up to date with your tetanus shots, bubblehead." I said as I helped pull the hook out of his mouth. Just as the hook came out, he smiled with a big drunken grin and you could see all the green, bullhead skin which was still stuck in his teeth. This sent me over the edge and I had to walk away with hopes of not pissing myself from laughing so hard.

When I finally came too, someone was poking me in the ribs telling me to get up. I sat up, looked around and realized that the poking had come from one of the two cops who were standing above me. "Wait, what!?" I asked out loud in a confused manor.
"Sorry to wake you Sir, but you were the easiest

to wake seeing as though you're sleeping on your tent and not in it." I stood up real quick and looked around... sure enough, I crashed right on top of my tent and slept like that for the whole night. A quick look at the tent door told me that I had obviously got into a fight with it and lost upon trying to gain entry. There was a big tear along side where the zipper was and a big melted patch where I must have held my lighter to it for some time in hopes of melting my way in. "Well, what do you guys need?" I asked the cops as I stretched nonchalantly. "We had a camp site at the end of the park get vandalized last night... someone stole their cooler and slashed their tires. The witness we have claims that it was a group of teenage kids who did it so we just wanted to let the park host know about it... this IS the park host's camp sight, is it not?" The officer asked with apparent disgust.

The "park host's" camp site was littered with beer cans, wood, bullheads, fishing poles, passed out bodies and various empty bottles of whiskey. On the side of my brother's camper (the park host's camper) was a big black scorch mark where it looked like someone hit it with a flame thrower. There was also a headless bullhead hanging off the beer can wind chimes which were hanging directly in front of the door.

"You may want to come back and tell the park host a little bit later... I'm pretty sure he's in no mood to deal with renegade teenagers right now..." I said frankly.

The two officers were also surveying the immediate area and must have decided that the park host wouldn't be helpful anyways. "Well, it's no big deal... we'll just go make the report in town and keep a closer eye on this park." The one officer said as the other tried to get control of his laughter. Wondering what he could be laughing at, I followed his gaze and saw what had the officer's attention. Jut was walking through the woods wearing a tight, short pair of pink yoga pants and a white, tank top belly shirt that came half way down to his belly button. "The bitch took me home, stole my clothes and left me alone in her room all night… this was all I could find to wear." Jut said as he casually walked up to the officers and I. "Ok Gentlemen, you have yourselves a fine day." said the one officer, trying to cover his laughter. They both got into their cruiser and drove off, laughing the whole way until you could no longer hear them. "Haters!" Jut said with displeasure. "Well, I suppose… let's clean this place up and wake the troops."

The camp was cleaned up, the drunks were scraped off the ground and everyone had some good breakfast in their bellies as we all sat around the fire discussing the prior night. We were supposed to have another derby that evening but decided against it once we seen multiple coast guard planes and helicopters flying up and down the river into the bay.

"I heard they're looking for survivors from a boating accident!" said someone who was walking down the road with his friend. "Yeah, I heard that a boat sunk last night and no one was found…"

"Well, when we went out fishing this morning, we picked up over three-hundred floating bear cans along the river… someone somewhere had a good time!"

A few of us around the fire started laughing and decided that the bullhead derby did get a little out of hand. Luckily for us, my brother was the camp host so there wasn't much that could be done about our shenanigans. Most everyone went back home that day for fear of being thrown into prison by the coast guard or from just being too sick from drinking.

"Should we have another derby next year?" I asked my brother and a couple others who were still sitting around. "Well… I'm thinking no… the campers here already avoid me like the plague and no longer even come to me with their camp ground problems… hell, I think that I've become the problem!" he said in response.

"Yeah… good call eh. Well, while were here… want a beer?" I asked my brother while digging into the cooler.

"Yeah, may as well… seeing as how we already cleared out most of the camp ground, what could possibly go wrong?"

"Excuse me, Sirs?" asked a man who walked out of the woods behind us. "My name is John from the Department of Natural Resources... may I have a word?

Walleye Derby Hero

Have you ever went ice fishing before? If not, let me break it down for you real quick.

Ice fishing consists of waiting until winter when there is enough ice on a bay / lake that you can walk or drive out into the middle of and fish. It's rather simple… all you need is an ice auger or something heavy enough to chip your way through the ice and into the water. Once you have your hole in the ice, you can use mini fishing poles to sit and jig for aquatic life such as walleye, perch, pike and so on. You can either sit on the ice out in the elements and jig or jig in style inside of an ice fishing shack. These shacks can be anything from a tent to homemade custom shack suited to the angler's needs. In my experience, it's better to use a shack over sitting outside in the elements with your teeth chattering in your head from the cold. Now that you have the basic understanding of ice fishing, allow me to tell you about a little tale which takes place on an icy wasteland in Northern Michigan.

The year was 2003 and my buddy Rod and I were gearing up for the annual walleye ice fishing derby. Being tall and rather skinny, Rod didn't drink quite as heavily like the rest of us Yoopers did eh. Instead, he just smoked a shit load of pot. "Fish shacks provide some of the best known shelters for clam baking!" he always said.

We managed to come across some extra money so we bought an ice fishing shack from one of our neighbors. It was a nice 6x8 shack with stud walls made out of 1x1s and wrapped in cardboard and tar paper. The floor was just a sheet of plywood with a couple 1x1 braces underneath of it for support. Needless to say, it was light weight and could be easily moved. It would have been even easier to move if we would have bought extra lumber to put runners on it so we could just drag it behind my 4-wheeler... but that would have required using money outside of our budget. Our budget was very strict and we had to use the left over money from buying the shack for needed supplies such as multiple 30pks of beer, a bag of weed and a shit load of cigarettes. "Eh, to hell with those runners!" I proclaimed to Rod as we were deciding on the best way to move our shack with my 4-wheeler. "This thing is light, right? We can lift it up with just the two of us, right? Well, all we need is a trailer or something to haul it around and I have just the thing!"

6:00 AM – The derby begins

There were an awful lot of confused people when

Rod and I came rolling up onto the edge of the bay with an ice shack, 4-wheeler, six 30pks, a duffle bag full of smokes and a boat trailer in tow behind the truck. People can understand the vast amounts of beer and tobacco while ice fishing but a boat trailer? This was new to them. No one said a word to us as we started loading the beer and tobacco into the shack after we hoisted it on top of the boat trailer. We then connected the boat trailer with the shack strapped to it to the back of the 4-wheeler. "You do realize that the water is frozen?" said one person off in the distance. "Hey, you lost your boat!" said another. "Those guys are high!" exclaimed yet another person as we mounted up on the 4-wheeler. "That we are sir! That we definitely are!" yelled Rod as I began to drive us out onto the ice.

There were people all over the place that day as

the derby was one of the Upper Peninsula's biggest ice fishing events. There were literally hundreds upon hundreds of ice shacks out on the bay with just as many people. We drove for about 20 minutes until I decided that we were in a good enough spot to fish. Being a little ways away from most everyone else and their shacks, we figured we would have a decent chance of catching something here. We drilled our fishing holes, got the shack settled onto the ice, fired up the heater and settled down to fish. I had a multipurpose radio / tv / headlight / siren thing that was mounted to the wall and received its power from a car battery that was on the floor. While I was messing with the tv and trying to fine tune the station into Regis & Kelly, (don't hate, it was the only station we had!) Rod was busy rolling up a fat one. Joint rolled, beers and fishing poles in hand, Regis and Kelly playing on the tv, we made a toast and settled into our seats with hopes of catching that hog of a walleye that would win us 1st place in the derby.

5:00 PM – Time to weigh in

"Walp, let's go weigh this dirty bastard to the weigh in tent!" Rod said through the cloud of smoke which engulfed the whole inside of the shack. He was referring to the one and only fish we had caught all day long, a little walleye barely even big enough to be considered a keeper. We got all suited up in our winter gear and waded through all the empty beer cans outside of the shack to the 4-wheeler. Almost reaching the 4-wheeler, I slipped on the ice and landed square on my back. Rod busted out in uncontrollable laughter as I lay on the ice likewise laughing. Maybe it was the weed, maybe it was the two whole 30pks we drank or maybe it was the flask of Canadian whiskey that Rod had brought... whatever the case was, we were hammered. Forgetting about the boat trailer even being hooked up to the back of the 4-wheeler, we drove as fast as we could to the weigh-in tent to get qualified and to see who was in the lead. Upon hauling ass onto shore with the wheeler, I drove right beside the tent only to take out 3 of the 5 guide lines used to keep the tent up with the boat trailer. It was a big heavy canvas Army tent which had about 80 people inside of it and we had just collapsed a whole corner on top of them. Being as drunk as we were, hysterical laughter ensued as we cracked another beer and walked towards the tent with our little walleye in hand. As soon as we walked in (first thing I noticed was that we were the only ones with beer in the whole tent) everyone in the tent stared at us... not one voice was to be heard as everyone just simply stared at us.

"So, what're you guys doin?" I asked the DNR officer who was weighing in walleye for the other anglers. Everyone immediately started laughing at us and our small fish while the DNR officer yelled at us for having alcohol in the tent.

"Fuuuuccccckkkkkkk youuuu." Rod said to the officer as he threw our little walleye at him with his left hand. The fish didn't even come close to hitting the officer… it just went sailing off into the corner where it was soon forgotten forever. Seeing that the situation was about to get a little out of hand, I grabbed Rod and we walked out of the tent to the 4-wheeler. No one followed us outside so I assumed they were just shaking their heads and were glad we left. As I fired up the wheeler and began to drive off, I once again forgot about the boat trailer and took out the other side of the tent's guide lines. With almost half the tent collapsed in opposing corners, we threw our empty beer cans onto the ice road and drove back to our shack while yelling "ALL HAIL THE BULLHEAD GODS!!"

9:00 PM – Lights! Fire! Action!
"Piss on those fish!" Rod said as he threw down his pole and fell over in his chair. "Yeah, I agree 110% man." I replied back while finishing off another beer and cigarette. We went outside to stretch and see if there was anyone else braving the cold winter night to stay out in their shacks and sure enough, there were a couple fires off in the distance. We loaded up a 30pk onto the 4-wheeler and decided to pay those distant fires a visit. We also took my little mutli-purpose radio and mounted it on the front of the wheeler so we could have some tunes while driving across the ice. At least, that's what we had intended to do

with the radio / tv unit but it was having some technical issues and the only thing that worked on it was the siren.

So there we were, flying across the ice in the blackness of night heading towards one of the only sources of light with the siren going as loud as possible. "FREEZE! DNR MOTHER FUCKER!" Rod yelled as we came up to his little cousin's shack. The door flew open and the kid came out with his hands up. "Give us all your beer!" Rod demanded through his face mask. The kid was trying to tell us that he had no beer but Rod kept cutting him off "Bullshit! I want a beer so you had better shit one out onto the ice!" You could tell that the kid was highly nervous over the whole situation as he didn't know who we were so I decided to step in and ease his worries. "Ok Kid, you've got til tomorrow afternoon to come up with a 30 pack. If not, we'll come back and sink your shack right where it sits so help us God! We're the DNR and we demand contribution to our fishing research!" With that being said, Rod threw his beer can and hit the kid square in the forehead. I fired up the wheeler and off we went. Siren still going, beer cans flying with boat trailer swaying back and forth, we were getting close to the fires we had seen earlier.

We were almost to the fire (which had many people gathered around it) when I hit a big pressure crack in the ice. The crack was pushed together and had ice chunks sticking up about 3ft which launched us up into the air and down onto our side. Helmets, beer cans, radios and car batteries went flying across the ice as the boat trailer unhooked and smashed into a nearby shack. "We're here!" I announced to Rod and everyone that had come running to our assistance. Luckily, we knew most of the people at the fire and they were likewise just as drunk. We gathered up all our shit which was scattered on the ice and caught up with the local derby gossip while hanging out at the fire. About an hour into drinking and carrying on, a pair of headlights came bouncing across the ice and was heading towards us at a high rate of speed. As the lights got closer, we could all tell that it was a white suburban or something similar and it was heading right towards the same pressure crack that I had hit. Upon hitting the pressure crack, the suburban got about 2ft of air and came crashing down onto the ice on all 4 tires but was sent into a spin. Due to the high rate of speed which it was going, the suburban slid sideways into someone's shack, completely destroying it. Eight people piled out of the suburban and not one of them was sober. They had just got done explaining that they were all from the Lower Peninsula when all of a sudden, a shack about 100yrds from us exploded. There was literally a mushroom cloud of flames as the walls & roof were splintered and sent flying through the chill night sky. "Oh shit!" said one of the party goers "I forgot to turn off my heater! My candle was still going too!!" Apparently the man's heater had gone out and his shack had slowly filled up with propane. Once the shack got enough propane inside of it, the candle (which he left going for light when he came back) ignited the propane and blew his shack completely into splinters. After we were all done laughing at the shack explosion, the suburban all of a sudden drove off without any of its passengers!

"To hell with that piece of shit!" said the man who had originally drove the suburban to the fire. "That's my brother's *hic* ... my brother *hic*

……. My brother's truck! *hic*" with that being said, the man doubled over and started puking on his boots. One of the passengers then explained how the driver's brother let him take the suburban for a "test run" up to the Upper Peninsula for the weekend. It was a 2004 or 2005 test vehicle which was not even out on the market yet. As the man explained to us how priceless the vehicle was, it hit a big ass rock that was jutting out of the ice and flipped onto its side. A few of use drove over to the suburban to see how much damage was done to it. The mirror on the driver's side was ripped off and all the panels on the same side were smashed and dented beyond repair. The laptop which was hooked up to the engine had snapped off of the mount and was sent through the passenger window, smashing upon impact with the ice. The passenger tire was flat and was only hanging on by a break line while the motor had appeared to have its engine mounts busted as well. Needless to say, the whole vehicle was a loss. The driver had stuck a stick between the seat and the gas pedal then put it into gear and let it roam the frozen bay on its own free will.

"This looks like a good time to leave." said Rod who was smoking a joint. "We're short on beer and these trolls are retarded in the head!" I was inclined to agree with Rod... whoever said "never trust a troll" had that statement right on the money eh. As we were driving back to the fire to announce our departure, the fire all of a sudden went out. It had been burning so hot for so long that it finally melted its way through the ice and completely submerged itself in the water. "Good timing!" I told Rod as we pulled up to what was left of the fire. "Well, we're running low on beer so we're going to head back to the shack... good luck with the suburban guys. You're going to need it!" I said as we started to drive off. Upon reaching top speed on the 4-wheeler, we hit the same damn pressure crack in the same damn spot and got thrown off the wheeler onto our backs on the ice. As soon as I landed on the ice, the boat trailer made one big bounce and hit me square in the stomach, knocking the wind out of me. "DUDE! Are you ok!?" yelled Rod as he came running over to me. I was unable to answer him due to trying to catch my breath so he did what any man would do for his fallen buddy. He cracked open a beer and started dumping it on my face. Choking and hacking while finally getting my breath back, I couldn't help but laugh. "That's just our luck too!" I told Rod as we both sat there laughing. We managed to put everything back onto the wheeler and start driving to the shack again. About half way back to the shack, we looked behind us and noticed a huge fire. We didn't pay much attention to it at the time but come to find out later the next day, the trolls had set their suburban on fire to "dispose of the evidence".

1:00 AM – What should have been, wasn't. Once we got back to the shack, we were surprised to see that one of the set lines we left in the water had a fish on it! Rod was pulling in the line that the fish had pulled out while I lit up a smoke. After a couple minutes of fighting the fish, Rod had managed to bring it to the top of the hole. It was a nice walleye, about a 7 or 8 pounder and it was sure to place us in the top 5. "Phillip, reach down and grab that prick!" Rod said with a big drunken cheesy grin on his face.

As I was reaching down to grab the fish, I flicked my cigarette into the hole and the damnedest thing happened…. The cigarette (still lit) hit the fishing line and melted it completely allowing the walleye to swim away unhindered. As I sat there still bent over ready to grab the fish which was no longer there, Rod started laughing. "Just our fucking luck!" he said as he reached over to grab another beer. "So long prize money, it would have been nice eh." Rod said while cracking open his beer. I began to laugh and started shaking my head in disbelief. "I can't believe that just happened… what in the HELL was that all about!?" I asked Rod. "Eh, to hell with it. We've got plenty of time to catch another one." he said just before he fell out of his chair and crashed through the door outside onto the ice. "What a hell of a first night" I thought as I sat there watching Rod try to pick himself off of the ice.

"Oh well, there's always tomorrow I guess… tomorrow will be the day. The day where we catch that hog walleye again and win our thousand dollar prize!" As Rod gathered his self into the shack, the alcohol finally began to take over my consciousness and I drifted off into an alcohol induced slumber.

The rest of the weekend went by fairly well eh. We managed to drink the six 30pks we brought out with us plus another one a buddy of ours brought out to us for reinforcements, smoke a half oz of weed and go through a carton of Marlboros. Oh yeah, we didn't catch any more fish that weekend either. We had decided just to hide out in the shack for the rest of that weekend for fear of being crucified by the DNR for taking out the weigh-in tent… plus there was a burnt, white suburban on its side which had yet to be explained to anyone in authority. Rod and I figured we would be the ones blamed for that even though we didn't have anything to do with it. This also helped us decide to just remain in the shack rest of the derby. Besides, it's dangerous out there on that frozen wasteland… there's people with boat trailers and beer!

What are friends for?

I remember when I was around 14 years old and Dentis talked me into staying the night at his house. I managed to convince my parents to let me stay over at Dentis's for movies but the truth was, we were going out partying. There was Dentis, Fatious and I and we were ready to rip up the town on this particular Saturday night. None of us had a driver's license so we had to hoof it a few miles to get some beer at Fatious's Dad's house. After seeing he only had a 12pk in his fridge, we started to dig deeper and eventually found a 5th of Popov Vodka. Popov is by far the worst, cheapest and most harsh vodka anyone can buy. Fatious's dad drank it though, why couldn't we?

So we headed off to the house that we were partying at for the night and proceeded to play the game of drink. It wasn't long before we went through the 12pk and tore into the vodka. I was already half boozed up when we opened the vodka so I figured it wasn't going to take much of it to do me in. This was the first time I had ever drank vodka so I wasn't quite sure what to expect and… my God! Was I in for a surprise!

As soon as I opened up the bottle, I took a big swig of it and nearly puked on the table. "This shits awful!!!" I exclaimed. Of course, we had nothing for a back either so I was stuck with drinking that God awful substance straight. A few minutes after that first initial swig, I began to feel terrific! I remember grabbing the bottle and holding onto it with a death grip as if I was never going to let it go again. "This shit ain't shit!" I yelled as I chugged. "It's like drinking water! WOOOHOOOOOOOOO!!!!!" I was really getting into the spirit of drinking when Fatious whipped out a little baggie and grabbed a beer can. I was thoroughly intrigued by this as I've never seen anything like it in my life. "What the hell are you doing MacGyver?" I asked Fatious with a dumbfounded expression on my face. "Making a peace pipe you damn Frenchman!" I really had no idea what the hell he was talking about so I just sat there and watched. After he was done crafting the makeshift bowl and packed it full of green, he handed it to me and ordered me to take a hit. I took a big hit from the beer can while Ty was holding the lighter and began to choke. Mind you, Fatious and I were 14 at the time and I had never smoked dope a day in my life let alone seen any until that night. What happened next… well, what I remember of it wasn't all that good eh.

Ever have the spins? People who drink a lot of alcohol over a short period of time and then smoke a bunch of pot usually get them really, REALLY bad. I remember laughing, stumbling everywhere I went and then everything went black. I completely blacked out for the next couple hours due to way too much vodka and pot. I was supposed to spend the night at Dentis's house but apparently that never panned out...

I remember walking down the hallway of my own house, leaning against the wall for support and knocking every single family portrait off the wall. I vaguely remember hovering over the toilet puking and making enough noise to wake the dead with my Mom yelling at me at the same time. "YOU'RE DRUNK!!!!" she yelled at me. "I AM NOT!!! *gag* ARRRGGGGGGG *puke* AHHHHHH!!!! *gag*". Ever have one of those pukes where your whole body stiffens up harder than the lips of a woodpecker and you're puking so hard that it sounds like you're screaming at the toilet? Yeah, that was me. I remember telling her that I wasn't drunk but there was obviously no way to hide it. Everything was spinning so fast in my vision that all I wanted to do was lay on the ground, dig my hands in the dirt and pray to the Bullhead Gods that I didn't fall off the earth. I must have made quite a commotion when I entered the house to wake up my mother. Other than wiping out the pictures on the wall and puking in the bathroom, I don't remember anything else that happened that night.

The next morning I woke up off the floor (I was

completely naked and covered in puke) got dressed and walked out into the living room like nothing happened. I kept wondering to myself if it was all just a bad dream and if my mother really was yelling at me that night. All my wondering was put to rest when my Mom seen me and tore me a new asshole verbally. I really wasn't paying attention to what she was saying as she was spitting and sputtering with rage that I was all fucked up. At the end of her little rant, she looked at my dad (who was also in the room with us) and said "Isn't that right Dale!?" He just looked at me, laughed and walked out. Apparently he got a kick out of hearing me puke and lie about not being drunk to my mother.

I called up Dentis to ask him just why the hell I didn't end up at his house after my ass chewing from Mom. "Well, after you took a few rips off the beer can and polished off your jug of vodka (as soon as he said vodka, I started dry heaving) you grabbed some chicks boobs, tried doing some pushups which only succeeded in you doing a belly flop on the cement which must have hurt because you then ran outside and puked for 45 minutes straight." I laughed a little bit because I had no memory of any of the things he stated happening to me that night. When I told him that I was grounded for a month due to him bringing me to my house instead of his, all he said was "What are friends for?"

Plight of the bird watchers.

So there I was, sitting in my brother's yard all bundled up in my Carharts, drinking beer and waiting for something to shoot at like I did every day at that point in time. It was early November of 04' and I was laid off for the winter with nothing but time on my hands so drinking beer and shooting critters out of season became a sport for me. One day out of the ordinary, I saw a van stop on the corner by the house. No one ever stops at that corner... "That's no damn good." I thought as I sat there and watched them. Low and behold, it was a group of bird watchers. Six of their kind rolled out of the van like they owned the place and started setting up stands for their cameras. Apparently there was some kind of rare owl that comes down from Canada every few years out in the field. It was a couple feet tall and almost jet white, quite the regal looking creature actually. I didn't blame them much for wanting to take some pictures of it but they kept blocking the whole corner! For about 4 days straight they kept on that corner like leaches, blocking traffic and being pricks. Finally I had enough. That's my corner and I'll be damned if some batch of bird watching dicks are going to take it over! So later that night, hours after they had driven off and it was dark, I walked out into the field to carefully place my new secret weapon.

My neighbor had a 3ft tall plastic owl lawn ornament and I managed to barter it off of him for some fresh venison and walleye. The owl was a light shade of grey and had little patches of darker grey spread all over it. Once I eyed up what I thought was about 200yrds from the road,

I hung the owl up from a nearby tree and just covered up enough that it'd take the watchers a little bit of time to see it the next day. After I had it setup just the way I wanted it, I headed back to the house and went to bed with a big grin on my face.

It was about 9:30am that next morning when the bird watchers had arrived and set up their wall of cameras that clogged up the whole corner. They were there for about 15 minutes before one of them had finally noticed the illusive owl sitting in the trees. They all repositioned their cameras and were just getting zoomed in to the owl when something happened they will never forget.

Right in front of their very eyes, that newly introduced synthetic owl species which they had never seen before exploded into pieces and vanished into thin air. I had put the owl in a place where not only they could see it but I could see it as well. The angle I had was just right as my viewing lane to the owl was leading away from the group. Needless to say, when a .308 round connects with a big ass frost covered plastic owl, it makes for quite the show! It literally shattered into pieces and completely disappeared into what little snow there was, lost from the site of the bird watchers.

Terror I believe would be the best way to describe what they were feeling. They didn't even bother to put the cameras into their cases; they just chucked them into the back of the van. They all piled into the van and took off out of there like a bat out of hell.

They were never seen again.

Night of the DUI

It was a Thursday night a few years back and the local town was kicking off their "Community Days" celebration that they have every year. The Thursday night wasn't packed with many events like there were on the following nights but it did have a couple. One of them was the volunteer fire department's softball game which has been held every Thursday night prior to the Community Day's weekend for years. I somehow managed to get suckered into announcing the event three years prior when I was all boozed up watching the game. I had my own little table with a microphone and a big speaker to broadcast my commentary across the immediate area. I usually started pounding beers as soon as I got there and was usually pretty tore up once the game was over. There wasn't much to announcing the game, you just announce each player as he or she got up to bat, say who caught the ball and toss in the occasional pun once in awhile. The puns usually revolved around balls and such or I'd make a statement like: "If a fire breaks out, we're in the safest place possible" or "Hey you! Make yourself useful and go get me another beer!" People loved it at any rate. As usual, when the news paper came out the next day, they would have a recap of the night and mention that "C.L. Phillip was announcing the game" which was always pretty neat to see. As long as my name wasn't in police & fire I was always happy to see it in the paper.

After our team got their asses handed to them with a score of 6 – 29 we all gathered to drink a few beers and bullshit for awhile. It was then, around 8:00pm when Billdo called my cell phone.

I had already been drinking for about three hours and had a very good buzz going on. Billdo was spewing promises of tire fires, women and beer into my ear. "Dude, go get your truck and meet me in town and then we'll go show'em how it's done!" I had the wander lust extremely bad this night and Billdo's promises of great partying time were more than enough to make me want to go. I slammed what was left of my beer, hopped on my new bike I had at the time and sped home to retrieve my truck.

When the switch was made for the truck I seen Speedstick walking down the road like he always did and convinced him to come along for a good night of fun.

Speedstick was the neighborhood slave. He had no job and didn't do anything other than play Nintendo so we took it upon ourselves to help him out by demanding that he do our bidding else never do anything with us again. He was a nice enough guy. He just didn't have skills at all nor was he the sharpest tool in the shed. Thus, he was the perfect man for the job of doing anything and everything we told him to do. Speedstick was especially proud of the new beer helmet he had just bought and was all about testing it out. We stopped at the local store to pick up more beer and smokes for the half hour ride into town. On our way there, I had managed to talk another one of my friends into coming along, Marie. Marie was quite the beauty and I was pretty surprised that I even talked her into coming along with us. Her boyfriend was out of town that weekend and apparently, she was itching to do something fun. Needless to say, she was more than excited to go hang out in town with us for the night and get her drink on.

I couldn't help but feel like something was going to go wrong that night. I was already boozed up, my truck only had one headlight (which was lost the weekend before when a mailbox suddenly leapt out in front of me) and I was going to pick up Billdo of all people. Whenever Billdo and I got together there was no excuse for the way we would act. With no regard for any laws or morals ever conceived, the two of us fed off each other to see who could out do who. So far Billdo was in the lead of mishaps with a drunk driving that he had received a couple weeks before. He was unable to drive, hence the reason I had to go pick him up in the first place. Once we got to Billdo's residence I called him up to let him know of our arrival.

"Yeah yeah, hold on a sec. Let me finish this beer, find my shoes and I'll be out in a sec." he said rather impatiently.

"Hey you asshole! I have the truck! I have the power! You got 1 minute to get the hell out here before the Drunk & Disorderly (the name of my truck) leaves your non-license haven ass here!" I told him bluntly over the phone as I hung up on him.

A couple minutes later he hopped in the truck and we started discussing what and where our objective was. Being as though there were three of us packed into the little Dakota with one riding in the back, I knew for a fact that something bad was going to happen that night. Honestly, I really didn't give a shit. I already had a 12pk dominated with a 30pk on ice in the back of the truck. That image alone was more than enough to entice the sinister drunkenness which was about to take place.

Billdo instructed that our destination lay within

one of the City Pits which were only accessible by 4-wheeler trails. "No problem" I said to my passengers' semi slurring my words. We were going about 50 when we hit the big sand embankment that was built for people to jump over the gate with their machines. Everyone's beer that he or she was holding hit the ceiling of the truck so hard that they crumpled and the beer shot around inside the truck as if a water sprinkler was on full blast. Marie had somehow turned upside down on the floor of the truck while Billdo had managed to stub his neck on the roof of the truck. Speedstick on the other hand who had volunteered to ride in the back of the truck for this alcohol powered joy ride was catapulted off of his feet landed belly first in the back of the truck so hard that he knocked the wind out of himself. When Speedstick made initial contact with his guts in the bed of the truck, the

truck had just landed nose first into the sandy trail. As soon as the truck nose dived it had sent Speedstick forward with such force that his new beer helmet exploded into pieces completely crushing his two beers shooting the liquid up into the air as if they were a champagne bottle exploding. As the truck came to a complete stop on the trail and we all adjusted our selves while surveying the scene, Billdo stared at me with tears in his eyes from laughing so hard. "Did you see Speedstick's circus show back there!?"
"You don't have to tell me man, I saw it all!" I said while likewise laughing. Marie didn't see it so we had to reiterate what had happened to her. Still laughing while trying to tell Marie what happened, Speedstick walked up to the window rubbing his head.

"Jesus jumped up Christ! Do you think we were going fast enough? You asshole!" Speedstick said with obvious anger. "You two pricks owe me a new beer hat!"

"Like hell we do!" Billdo said still laughing at him. "We didn't make your ass ride in the back, you volunteered!"

"Just hop back in and I promise I'll go easy from here on out Speedstick" I told him still wiping tears of laughter from my eyes. "I'm not sure where exactly we're supposed to go but I think we should keep this bitch rollin' and hope we don't get buried in this deep ass sand." With a look of extreme displeasure on his face, Speedstick opened another beer and jumped back in the truck.

We drove down the trail for another ten minutes or so before we saw the fire that marked the party. Once I found a suitable place to park the truck, we grabbed our cooler of beer and started the trek through the sand to see who all was at the party. There were 20 – 30 people or so standing around the fire and only a small fraction of them had drinks. We began to realize that something was terribly out of place...

"What the hell Billdo?" Marie yelled. "These people are like 15 years old! They're all kids!"

"Bullshit!" Billdo retorted although he knew that Marie was right.

"Actually, we're all 16 and 17 thank you very much" one of the teens said in her defense.

"Good job Billdo. Your big party that you were so hyped up for is a high school party! You wouldn't by any chance have some kind of a grand scheme to rob the cradle now would you?" I said teasingly. "Either you were majorly misinformed or your scary ass is turning into a pedophile!"

"Well what the hell do you propose we do now then? Huh smart guy?" Billdo demanded and was obviously getting pissed at the situation.

By this time, the alcohol was in full command of my body and mind so I spoke the first thing that came into my head...

"To the bar!" I yelled.

"To the bar!" Billdo, Speedstick & Marie all yelled in unison.

"You guys suck. We want to go too!" one of the girls said as we started to walk off. "Not my fault you're like 12." Billdo said looking back over his shoulder. "Give me a call when your 18 and I might think about it. That is if you're old enough to even know what I'm talking about."

"Screw you!" she screamed at Billdo as we walked off laughing at the teen's misfortune.

We walked back to the truck, tossed the cooler (and speedstick) in the back and saddled up for the dangerous drive into the heart of the city.

We were driving out of the sandpit and into the heart of town. Our mission was to head to the bars and bring a conclusion to this night of debauchery in an epic sort of way. I drove us to one of the downtown bars and once we arrived, we had two hours left to play. I don't really remember much about being in the bars but I do remember that I was really drunk eh. Once the bars closed down, I made sure we had everyone in check (Billdo, Marie and even Speedstick) and then we made a run to the last place on our checklist: Taco Bell.

Ah yes, Taco Bell. The final destination for most all drunks who manage to close down the bars after a good night of drinking down town. I was driving pretty decent from what I remember and Taco Bell was on the horizon. We were so close to it that I could taste those Mexican pizzas when all of a sudden, cherries and berries appeared behind us!! The thought to flee came suddenly but I quickly disregarded the notion as this would only make the situation worse. I pulled over directly in front of taco bell and when I did, multiple friends of mine who happened to be sitting in the window noticed my truck and began pointing and laughing. My heart sank to the soles of my shoes as I knew I was about to get my first ever DUI. As the officers got out of their cruiser and started walking towards the front of my truck, Speedstick (who I had completely forgotten about) sat straight up in the bed of the truck and asked in a drunken stupor "What's going on??" Both cops jumped back and reached for their guns. As soon as their hands went for their guns, Billdo shouted out the passenger window "SHOOT'EM! SHOOT'EM!! SHOOT HIM!!!!!"

At that moment, my sorrow turned into complete and utter laughter. I had totally forgotten about Speedstick being in the back and Billdo's comment made me laugh like hell. When the female officer came up to the window of my truck, I had tears falling off my cheeks from laughing so hard. "License and registration please" The female officer said. I handed her what she wanted and all I could say was "You got me" through tear filled eyes while still laughing.

I passed all the sobriety tests they gave me and when she said "Ok, now I need you to blow into this." I replied with "This is where I now fail your test." She was rather nice about the whole ordeal and I almost had her talked into driving me through taco bell but alas, she had other things to do that night. They wanted to give Marie a citation for back talking an officer of the law but I talked them out of it as they had already caught the big fish with a DUI. At least they granted me the request and I was able to get Marie off the hook.

They took me to jail and lodged me for the night in the drunk tank. The next morning, I woke up on the cement floor to one of the turn keys asking me if Billdo could get the keys to my truck. "Are you fucking serious?" I asked in confusion.

"Yeah. He's here and would like the keys to your truck. He said he'll be back later to pick you up once you're released." The officer said.

At first, I thought it was a trick. Two weeks prior, Billdo himself was sitting in this same exact cell with the same exact turnkey officer working the doors. Imagining the trap that they were going to set for Billdo to nail him with a driving without a license citation, I told them "Go ahead. I could use the company in here anyways." The officer looked at me with a raised eyebrow and suspicion for a few seconds before walking off. As the officer walked down the hallway, I smiled to myself and said out loud: "What are friends for?"

Assholes and shenanigans, adventures in camping.

Every Memorial Day my family and friends always go to camp at the local park. It was the Friday before Memorial Day and I just picked up Fatious Maximus so he could help me set up camp at the park. This weekend was going to be a weekend like no other eh. We had seven thirty packs of Busch light's finest brew in back of my truck along with a half ounce of some very fine greenery and a couple bags of chips. After we had spent all of our money on the booze, drugs, tobacco and some much needed tiki torches we had just enough money left to buy 2 bags of Doritos which were on sale at the local Wal-Mart. We were to be camped at the park from that Friday night until the following Monday and decided that 2 bags of chips would be plenty of food for the weekend. After all, there's a pork chop in every can of beer so we knew we wouldn't starve to death.

Upon reaching the park, Fatious hopped out to help me back in my camper into our camping spot. While he was waving me back he failed to mention that I was a little too close to one of the numbered posts and it busted in half when I backed over it. "No big deal" I thought as Fatious was doubled over in a drug induced laughing frenzy. "The DNR will fix it... after all, that is what they are paid to do". Once we got the camper all set up with the canopy all rolled out and our two dozen tiki torches all set up, we smoked another fatty and opened another beer. Nothing too exciting happened that night as most everyone was just getting all settled into the camp ground and set up for our long weekend of depravity and self bodily abuse.

It was around 8 the next morning when I awoke to my whole camper shaking and shit falling off the table. The first thing I noticed was that Fatious had passed out in the same bed as me, had his arm around my waist and had a half ate hotdog bun with chips inside of it hanging out of his mouth. On the other side of the camper were Billdo and another body that I didn't recognize. As I began to become more aware of the situation, I slapped Fatious in the head and then realized that the view outside of the window was speeding by! Dentis had hooked onto my camper and was dragging it down the road. He was going to haul us to the dump and leave us there. After a bunch of yelling and bad noise, he finally stopped and we hauled my camper back to the camping spot. He had only dragged us a little way down the road but he definitely was one up on me in the shenanigan department for the weekend.

A little later that afternoon, I went back to my house to grab my boat and decided to go fishing. Dentis had asked me to take his nephew fishing for the day because he really had the walleye fever and Dentis had no way of taking him out. I agreed to the idea and along with Dentis's nephew Stubby, Fatious and Fucken Todd, we headed out to the vast waters of the bay to slay the illusive walleye. Stubby was the average good kid around the age of 13. He loved to hunt and fish and couldn't seem to get enough of it. Todd on the other hand… he was an asshole. He was good company to have around but would go behind your back to hit on with your girlfriend any chance he got. He couldn't help it though; he just loves women in general. He earned the nick name "Fucken Todd" by always being sneaky and trying to steal everyone's girlfriend. Despite his unnatural lust towards women, he was still a decent guy and a ton of fun to have around. We had a couple 30 packs with us along with a couple dozen worms and 4 or 5 busted up fishing poles (they were broken due to the bullhead derby). Once we got into the bay and set the boat adrift, we cast out a couple poles with no cares as to whether or not we caught any fish. The only thing we were after (except Stubby) was to catch a nice tan and an even nicer buzz. About 2 hours into our expedition Fatious had remember something about a date he was supposed to go on and requested that we bring him back. I granted his request and piloted us back to the park.

Waving goodbye and throwing lead head jigs at Fatious as we left, Todd and I along with Stubby decided we hadn't had enough of fishing and drinking yet so we idled back down the river. We were also searching the mainland for another recruit to replace Fatious who had obviously never heard of the expression "bros before hos". Half way up the river we were flagged down by a familiar face that was in some thick brush... it looked like he was taking a shit. I wheeled the boat around and beached us on shore to see who the hell it was. We heard a voice yell "Are you guys goin fishing!?"

"You're damn right!" I replied, half boozed up. "Do you got room for one more?" asked the man who was still shitting in the woods.

"Sure do!" Todd said and then immediately looked back at me and asked "Who the hell is that?" I really didn't know who we were talking to either so I had no answer. But within 30 seconds we found out

The sun was blotted out from the sky and we felt the boat shake when this mammoth of a man came walking towards us. Of all the people to run into on this day of play, Ranson was standing before us in all of his glory and inhumanity. Now Ranson is the type of guy who will sit straight up in bed each morning, hate everything and then reach for whatever booze is left over from the night before and start drinking it within minutes of opening his eyes. Needless to say, he fit right in with the rest of us.

"I'm sorry I don't have much beer with me.... but if I can have some of your beer I'll give you this bottle of fire water." Ranson said earnestly. "Sure!" Todd and I both said at the same time. When he hopped in the boat he nearly capsized us with his enormous size and Stubby made a couple squeaks of displeasure when we ordered him to sit next to Ranson. "Just don't eat Dentis's nephew and we will have a good time out there eh." I jeered at him. "Ah. Fat jokes... thanks dick." he said with while flipping me the finger.

The bottle Ranson had given to us in exchange for some beer was not just some fire water... it was a whole gallon of firewater! "Where the hell did you get this from!?" I asked him once we had gotten into the bay and back at the fishing game. "I dunno... somewhere around the house or something... the fuck should I know?" He said with a half boozed up expression.

"Well, at least it's in safe hands now eh" Todd said, eyeing it up eagerly. Once we got back out into the bay and set the boat adrift once again, he and I decided to see how fast we could make the bottle of fire water disappear. After all, The Bullhead Gods hate cowards and we were far from cowards.

It was about an hour or so from sun set and the gallon was almost gone. Ranson, Todd and I were completely wasted and it wasn't even dark yet. All I knew at this point in time was that I had two or three more hours left before my body gave up and passed out on me. And that I still had stubby with me. "HEY!" I screamed at them to make sure everyone was still awake.

"WHAT!" Todd screamed back as he choked on a pull of firewater.

"Ok then. Pull.... uhm... Do something with your poles because we need to get back to the park before we all get violent and drown each other." As I fired up the mariner and started to drive us back towards the mouth of the river, the large amount of booze in my system clenched hold of my being and forced me to take a little snooze.

The next thing I recollect, someone kicked me off of my seat and I fell over the side of the boat.

But when I fell over the side of the boat... I landed on solid ground.

"What the......hell?" I stood up and observed my surroundings with an astonished look on my face. "Are you serious Phillip!?!?" Todd yelled at me. "What.....what the hell happened?" was all I could ask while still trying to comprehend what had just happened. Stubby was over in a little patch of weeds laughing so hard that I thought he was going to piss his pants while Ranson was bitching about being too drunk for this. "You hit a damn island you asshole!!!" Todd said as he tripped on a stump and fell on his ass.

"It's not just an island Louie, it's the only island in the bay!" Stubby said still laughing crazily. Apparently I had passed out while driving the boat and launched us on a grassy, sandy island. Luckily nobody got hurt but then again how could you get hurt when there is nothing but weeds and sand on the island. The sad part was that no one else even noticed we were heading towards the island! Stubby said he did but he didn't want to say anything because it looked like I was enjoying my alcohol induced nap. Once we got back into the boat and shoved off from shore, we hurried up and sped off to the campground so Stubby could tell his dad about the fish he caught.

We were half way back to camp when we came across Stubby's dad who was at another camp ground visiting some friends. We stopped and let stubby out so he could show his dad all the fish he caught then we sped off back down the river without him.
"Now that we're kid free, let's get crazy!" Todd said as he spilled the beer he was holding all down the front of him.

"You got it!" I replied back. My brave gauge was running at maximum power and I was feeling pretty damn good. Upon entering the area of the boat launch, we noticed four other boats were lined up waiting for their turn to load up. "We ain't gots time for this shit!" I yelled while speeding up the motor. "All hands, brace for impact!"

We hit the river bank right next to the boat launch at full speed and we went sailing into the woods as the other boats and on lookers sat there watching in horror. Beer cans, worms and fishing pole parts went flying into the air as we glanced off of a stump and came to a stop. "All hands! Prepare to abandon ship!" I yelled after I sat myself upright.

"Aye aye captain!" said Ranson as he threw the anchor at a tree a couple feet away from the boat. The three of us gathered up what was left of our booze and began to make our way back to camp despite the horrified looks of everyone who had just witnessed the event.

"Those guys are fucked up!" I heard someone say behind us as we staggered down the road.

We entered the camp site with about as much flair as a mute trying to sing the National Anthem. Ranson tripped over a log, fell flat on his face and couldn't get back due to the alcohol finally taking over his consciousness. Todd walked up to the first girl he saw and pretended to trip over his own two feet so he could go face first into a set of boobs... fucken Todd... I was in rare form as well and decided that it was time to get back at Dentist for his antics earlier that morning. I walked up to one of the tiki torches and yanked it out of the ground.

"Hey Dentis! Think fast!" I yelled as I over hand swung the tiki torch. The can which held the lamp oil dislodged from the top and went sailing way up in the air. About the time the can stopped gaining altitude, the top of it came off and all of the oil began to dump out and catch fire in mid air. A thick blanket of flaming tiki torch oil came raining down on Dentis's tent, fully engulfing it in flames.

"Joke's on you sucker! That's not even my tent! I borrowed it from Billdo!!" he yelled and immediately doubled over in laughter.

"That damn thing cost me a hundred and thirty dollars!" Billdo yelled while running towards his flaming tent. He managed to go inside and get the only thing he was worried about; his cooler full of booze. The only other thing in there was a sleeping bag which Dentist had borrowed from me initially so; it wasn't too big of loss. After we all watched the tent melt into a big ball of plastic from the fire, Billdo looked at me and said; "Yer gunna get it!"

We came to drunken terms that he could give me one punch anywhere besides the face as compensation for his tent burning down. Instead of punching me in the stomach or chest like I had thought he was going to do, he kicked me square in the balls. Before the pain set in and I fell onto the ground, I managed to get one good swing in with the tiki torch across Billdo's back.

Let me just say; there's a reason why the Chinese used bamboo poles to torture people.

The end of the pole was frayed into five smaller strips of bamboo and when the pole made contact with Billdo's back, it cut through his coat, shirt and struck his bare skin. Five big bleeding gouges were left in Billdo's back from the bamboo pole and we both hit the ground at the same time, moaning in pain. I was holding my balls and he was wiggling around with his back arched up in the air screaming like someone had shot him. Everyone else just stood around laughing at us and eventually left us to defend ourselves against each other.

"Time out!" Billdo said as soon as he was able to quell the pain in his back.

"Yeah, good call." I said as the stomach ache feeling came over me after a man takes blunt trauma to the balls.

We sat up and stared at each other for a few seconds, glanced over where his tent used to be then I followed his gaze to my camper. "I get the good bed!" he said as he stood up.

"Ah, fuck it. Yeah I suppose. You can have the good bed… just don't go and bleed all over the damn thing eh." I said to him as I picked myself off the ground. Feeling beat up and being entirely way too drunk, we decided to call it a night.

I woke up the next morning to some giggling and a shutting of the front door. I knew something was happening but I was way too tired and hung over to give a shit. Just as I was about to drift off to sleep again, I got the sudden feeling that I had strep throat. My throat was hurting so bad that I started to choke and gag some. Forcing me to get up and look around, I noticed Billdo sleeping on the comfortable bed and he was likewise coughing and choking. There was a thick haze in the air and I suddenly realized what had happened. Dentis and Fatious took a fire extinguisher, shoved it through the door and sprayed it inside of the camper for a good minute or two while Billdo and I slept. The entire inside of the camper was full of a thick, chalky haze and everything was covered in the white substance from the extinguisher. We both ran out of the camper only to come face to face with Dentis and Fatious who were laughing like hell.

"That's twice I've got you!" Dentis said, pointing at me and laughing.

I didn't even say anything in reply. My head was hurting so bad that all I did was walk to my truck, lock the doors and go back to sleep. I heard some commotion just as I was about to fall asleep and jumped up real quick to see what was going on. Fucken Todd, who had been up all night long without any sleep, was driving down the road with his pop-up camper in toe and still had it fully assembled. I looked just in time to watch a low hanging branch catch the top of his pop-up camper and tear the whole thing completely off. I started to laugh but immediately started dry heaving due to my head pounding so badly. All I heard was laughter and yelling as

Todd kept driving down the road. I laid my head down only to have Billdo come knocking on the window. "Can I come in?" he said through bloodshot eyes.

"No but you can sleep in the back... the top has a lock on it." I replied through the window.

"Thanks... My back is really, really sore..."

"Yeah, I flayed you open like a fish with that tiki torch bamboo pole last night."

"Ah, yes. I forgot about that..." Billdo said in reflection. "Too bad Dentist wasn't in the tent when you burned it to the ground eh."

"That's no shit! The inside of my camper is destroyed... we need to get that asshole back somehow." I replied.

"Oh we will... but first, I need some more sleep." Billdo said as he went to the back of the truck and hopped in with a pillow and blanket. Seeing that no one else was going to mess with me immediately, I put in some earplugs, laid myself back down and began to drift off to sleep.

Dreams of practical jokes on Dentist involving flaming tiki torches and fire extinguishers fluttered through my head as I slept.

Customers like us - I

"Well thank you very much ma'am!" I said to the obviously gay man who had just got done setting up my account. I had just moved and figured that I needed somewhere to stash my money from myself so I wouldn't spend it all at the bars. I decided that I would confide my trust with Stupid Bank as a lot of my friends said they were pretty good. What I didn't stop to think about was the fact that all my friends at the time had pretty deep pockets and never ran out of money like I was surely to do. As soon as I got home and started digging through my little packet of bullshit and lies they gave me, I noticed I had quite the spiffy looking balance book. It was to be used whenever I wrote a check or used my debit card. Being the financially responsible person that I am, I took that book and tossed it in the garbage. "Who needs that damn thing when your online account tells you all the purchases you've made!" I thought. Well, it never struck me that most charges didn't go through for a couple days and that the online account I always looked at was never truely up to date.

Within the first couple of months of banking with Stupid Bank I accumulated a few hundred dollars in over draw fees. One day in particular, I figured out that I had eight over draw charges to my account at $32.00 each. I found out after I went to buy a pack of Winstons and had my debit card denied right on the spot. "To hell with them! This time, it's personal!" I thought as I stormed out of the store without my much needed pack of smokes. I went directly home and made the call which would ultimately make me hate Stupid Bankwith an extreme passion forever.

After pressing numerous numbers on the dial pad, getting disconnected multiple times and wasting 45 minutes of my day, I was more than ready for the poor unsuspecting woman who finally took my call. "Yes is this about the account number ####?"

"Why yes it is."

"Ok. So, how may I help you today Mr. Phillip?" she said in a sweet voice.

"Well, you can start by explaining to me why I have EIGHT OVERDRAFT CHARGES AT THIRTY-TWO BUCKS A CRACK TO MY ACCOUNT!!!!!" There was a good 20 seconds of silence before the gal managed to clear her through and begin to explain.

"Well Mr. Phillip... you see..."

"YOU FUCKERS ARE ROBBING ME BLIND!!!" I yelled as I cut her off in mid sentence.

"Well Mr. Phillip, let's take a look at your spending habits, shall we?" She said without a trace of that sweetness she once had.

"Yeah, let's do that!" I said to her as I became even more pissed that she was no longer talking to me nicely.

It took a few seconds to pull up my spending records and when they finally came up, she began to talk to me as a mother would when chewing out her son over stupid shit.

"Well Mr. Phillip, you can start saving money by actually using our branch ATMs that will not charge you anything extra for taking out money. You've got over 40 dollars in charges for using non-Stupid Bank ATM machines." she said in a frank tone.

"Well maybe I would if you assholes actually had more than one machine in this whole town!"

"Sir, we've got three branches with three branch

ATMs at each one of their locations."

"Yeah, and guess what? None of those locations are anywhere near the bars I go to! Maybe if you cheap bastards had more than 3 machines in this damn place, I wouldn't have this issue! Ever think about putting one of your stupid machines inside of a bar?" I asked with extreme displeasure.

"Ever think about not drinking at those bars, period, Mr. Phillip? That would save you money as well." she said with a smug tone in her voice.

"Ok you bit…" I was immediately cut off by her as she kept on rolling with her accusations.

I'm also showing here that you've got a consistent, daily charge of $8.29 at the breeze inn station… are you a smoker Mr. Phillip?" she asked while still being smug.

"Why does it matter if I smoke or not!?! I called you to get my damn account straightened out, not be judged for smoking by some snobby bitch!" I said as my patience was quickly dissolving.

"Let me guess Mr. Phillip, you do not use the little balance book that was given to you in your startup packet?" she asked with pleasure.

"Well no! Why the hell would I waste my time penning in my spending when all I have to do is look at my online account??" I asked as my knuckles turned white from gripping my phone so hard. I was also thinking back to when I threw that same little book she was talking about in the garbage.

"Hah... I mean... your online account is never an accurate way to check your balance Mr. Phillip. Sometimes it takes two through four days for a charge to go through especially if you're writing a lot of checks or even using your debit card. She said in a triumphant voice. The bitch knew she trumped me but I let out one last volley of screaming before she laughed and hung up on me.

"WHY IN THE HELL WOULD YOU PROVIDE A SERVICE THAT OBVIOUSLY DOESN'T FUCKING WORK!!?!? DAMN YOU! I WANT MY MONEY BACK AND I WANT IT NOW!!!"

I realized that I was yelling at just my phone as she was no longer on the other end of the line. I was so mad at this point that I threw my phone as hard as I could at the ground only to have it strike my foot. Spitting and sputtering with rage, my face was beat red and my foot was throbbing in pain. I picked up the phone and hit redial (I was actually surprised it was still working) only to come ear to voice with that stupid machine that asks if I want English or Spanish even though we live in America. "ENGLISH! ENGLISH! FUCKING ENGLISH!" I yelled into the phone and then threw it out the door and over the balcony this time. The phone landed on the other side of the road and slid into the ditch. I sat on the couch and lit up a Winston butt from the ashtray as I thought back to everything that had just been said. After taking few minutes to cool off I started laughing. "I told my bank that they were robbing me blind..." I said out loud to myself with a grin.

Customers like us – II

The months started to pile up after the first encounter I had over the phone with the Stupid Bank gal and so did the overdraft charges. You could say it was my own fault for not paying attention to my spending but, hey, who likes to blame their self? Its way easier to blame the problem I had with over spending on my ability to drink the beers at a high rate of speed. You sit at the bar and drink till your cash is all gone so what do you do? You hit up the ATM for some more money eh. When it comes to drinking and spending money, there's just no such thing as enough. It's quite fun to walk up to the ATM, stick your card into it, lie to the girl your with about the size of your account and take out the maximum amount allowed. Once your account is at 0, the pending transactions from the previous days decided to all go through at once and leave you with multiple $32 overdraft fees. It's a vicious cycle and I always screwed myself with it.

One day I was sitting at home planning my night out on the town and decided to look at my online account to see what I had to spend. I immediately noticed that my savings account was no longer listed on the available accounts. This didn't really concern me at that point in time so I decided just to wait until the next day to figure it out. The next day after work, I went into the main branch office to talk with someone who could tell me what the hell was going on. Upon talking with the bank teller I learned that they got sick of me never having any money in my savings account so they closed it. Apparently, it cost me $10 a month to keep it open and since I never had any money in it, it would always go into the negative and add another fee. Her exact words were "You're not responsible enough to have a savings account." So, they gave me a second checking account. Yeah, that's just what I needed... another card to use when I was all drunk so I could rack up even more over draft fees. And guess what? I did just that eh. When one card failed to work at the bars, I would just bust out the other (my fall back account) to save my ass.

About two months into having two debit cards with two different checking accounts, I managed to accumulate over $600 in over draft fees. I finally decided enough was enough when I found out that they wouldn't allow my spending to go over $1,000 on either of my cards at one time. I was trying to buy a plane ticket so I could visit some family and the cost of the ticket was over $1200 so I was unable to buy it.

This was the day that my love/hate relationship blew apart at the seams with Stupid Bank.

I walked into the main branch office with a calm and collected demeanor expecting this to be a smooth operation. I waited in line for the bank teller and once I got up to her, I asked about possibly having my spending limit increased for just one day so I could buy the plane ticket. She was unable to help me. What she was able to do however was set me aside for 30 minutes until a personal banker was able to see me. Getting a little more disappointed with the entire situation, I sat there and waited for 35 minutes until the personal banker came and got me. We walked into her little room and I told her what I was trying to do.

"Yeah, I can see how this would be an inconvenience to you Mr. Phillip. Well, unfortunately, I can't help you. I'll have to get our manager and he'll be the one who can surely help you out. Can I have you sit in the lobby for a little bit longer?"

"...I suppose so." I muttered unhappily.

...another forty-five minutes later...

"Mr. Phillip? Hi there! Step into my office and we'll see what we can do to help you out." said a man with a slicked back, greasy haircut. I walked into the office and took a seat. Once again, I had to explain to him what I was trying to do.

"Yeah, I can see how this would be an inconvenience to you... unfortunately, I am unable to authorize such a request so I'll have to have you call this number and ask our executive manager." He said with a smile on his face. At this time, I was almost ready to come unglued but then he calmed the storm inside by handing me his phone.

"I can call him from here?" I asked rather puzzled.

"Yep, you sure can. Go right ahead and see if 'she' can help you out." He said still smiling. I took the phone and dialed the number he provided me with. After pressing 1 for English, 3 for assistance with something, 6 for an actual person, 3 again for the extension number and then inputting the twelve digit extension number itself, I was being connected to the girl I needed to talk to.

"Hello. Can I have the name and account number of who I am speaking with?" she asked with a pleasant voice. I gave her my information and she replied back "Please hold."

At this point in time, I managed to calm down a little bit as I was SURE this girl would be the one to give me what I wanted.

"Ok, back! Well Mr. Phillip, your account has been flagged for aggressive and vulgar behavior from your last discussion over the phone. I have to ask: are you going to be calm and civil today?"

"…well that depends. Are you going to give me what I fucking want!?" I snapped at her.

The regular manager who was sitting in the office with me still almost spit out his coffee when he heard me ask the question.

"Well, let's see what we can do but I do have to ask you to please refrain from swearing or else I'll be forced to hang up on you." She lectured to me. "So, how can I help you?"

I once again, for the third time, explained what I was trying to do. Once I got done explaining she sat on the other end of the phone line without saying anything for about thirty seconds.

"Unfortunately Mr. Phillip, we are unable to process your request. Upon looking back at your statements, you've proven that you are not responsible enough with your money and have too many over draft charges." She said frankly.

"So… let me get this straight… I've got over two thousand dollars in one of my two checking accounts and you're telling me that I can't buy a plane ticket?" I asked with extreme displeasure.

"That is correct sir."

"You mean… you aren't going to let me spend my own money?"

Well, it's not like that sir… you see, due to your history…"

"No, it's fucking EXACTLY like that!" I yelled into the phone. The manager who was still in the room with me damn near jumped right out of his chair when I exploded on the girl over the phone. At this moment in time, my face turned beat red and I was so mad that I couldn't even talk right. Spitting and sputtering with rage, I continued yelling into the phone.

"WHAT GOOD IS A BANK THAT WON'T LET ME SPEND MY OWN FUCKING MONEY!!!"

"SIR, if I may PLEASE explain!"

"NO! YOU CAN'T EXPLAIN! You bunch of dicks have earned damn near half of MY income through your bullshit overdraft fees! Seriously, do the math! Add up all those over draft fees then tell me that I do not deserve to buy a fucking plane ticket with my own damn money!" I continued yelling into the phone.

"SIR! I am very sorry but we cannot allow you to go over one thousand dollars per day!" she said with exasperation.

"Well you can go burn in hell then!! I'll go find a bank that WILL!" and with that, I slammed the phone down so hard that the plastic phone housing cracked. I then pointed at the manager who was standing in the corner of the office fearfully and said "Get ALL of my fucking money out of my goddamn checking accounts right NOW!"

"Ok Sir... just be calm and we'll go get your money..."

We then walked back into the main part of the building and he even had enough courtesy to bring me directly to the front of the line. Once we got to the bank teller, she looked at me and said "Hi there! How is your day going Sir?"

"Well, it would be a whole lot better if you assholes would let me spend my goddamn money!" I snapped at her.

"Oh... well then... ok..." she replied back.

"Yeah... this gentleman would like to close his account down." stated the Manager.

After a few minutes of button clicking and a swipe of one of my debit cards, I had just over two thousand dollars all laid out in front of me.

"Is there anything else I can help you with Sir?" she asked cautiously.

"Yeah. You can take these stupid fucking things..." I then took out both cards and threw them down on the counter "and shove them in the deepest, darkest corner..."

"Ok Mr. Phillip" the manager said as he cut me off. "It's been a pleasure and I must now ask you to leave."

"Gladly!" I said as the red in my face began to dissipate.

Just as I got to the main entry door, I stopped and turned around to take one last look at the rather nicely constructed bank.

"Damn bunch of thieves!" I hollered across the whole lobby. With those final parting words, I walked out of the building and didn't even look back to see if the manager was calling the cops. Honestly, I didn't even care if they would have called the cops or not! I was so utterly disgusted with them that it made me want to shit on one of their ATM keyboards. As I started driving down the road and lit up a Winston, I began to laugh at myself.

"Man, that felt GREAT!" I thought as I took a long, hard earned drag from my Winston.

I went to another local bank and described what had just happened not twenty minutes prior to my arrival. I also stated that "I am NOT above freaking out and causing a big scene in public." The bank teller looked at me with a likewise disgusted look and said "You can spend up to $5000 a day with us and it doesn't matter what kind of credit you have... what a bunch of dicks!"

"Perfect!" I said as I threw down my wad of hundreds. "Ma'am, I'd like to start an account with this fine bank!"

From there on out, my banking problems were

solved as this bank even had overdraft protection! They even let me have my own savings account along with a checking instead of just two checking accounts!

As I walked out of the bank with all my new information inside of a folder they gave me, I couldn't help but mutter the words one last time.

"...damn bunch of thieves."

The Jaeger Fueled Dynasty

"Wait, who's getting married and where?" I yelled at Jut, who was sitting in the passenger seat of my Dodge Dynasty. "Turn this damn death trap off so I can hear you!" he yelled back. Once we hit a dirt road that was suitable for conversing, I pulled over and shut down the ole' Dynasty.

You see, the Dynasty hard a pretty hard life which started about 6 months prior to this...which was also around the same time I purchased the magnificent machine from my parents. The dynasty's latest tragedy was from Billdo and I booze cruising down the road and placing a bet. The bet was whether or not I could straddle a piece of fire wood that was lying in the middle of the road with the Dynasty and not hurt anything.

Against my better judgment, I tried to drive over it.

It stood up on and end sheered the exhaust off at the firewall. The quiet dynasty was turned into a deafening, roaring beast that sounded like a whole fleet of monster trucks revving their engines at the same time. It was so loud that it shook the pictures on my brother's walls every time I drove up to his house. Needless to say, it was damn near impossible to have a conversation and drive at the same time.

"Oh this buddy of mine... you know'em too. He's getting married tonight and there's tons of free keg beer." Jut said enthusiastically. "Plus there's gunna be lots of sluts there, I can feel it!"

"Mmmm, keg beer. I love keg beer!" I said honestly. "That shit's so great. You grab that big ole' plastic red cup, fill'er up with some good cold foamy keg beer and drink it like water eh. It gets everywhere too! There's just no stopping it! You can't even breathe heavy without the shit flying all over yourself!" I was obviously starting to get pretty fired up about this whole discussion of keg beer and sluts. The timing was also right for earlier in the day I got paid for 80 hours of manual labor. Visions of keg beer and slutty bride's maids giving me lap dances while I held fists full of $10 dollar bills flooded into my head. "Ok Jut, we're going! You know where it's at? Ok, good. We'll go get slicked up some and head there around 8. Got any more beer?" and with that, I put in my ear plugs and fired up the Dynasty.

Around 8:30 that night, Jut and I rolled into the parking lot of the reception while keeping our heads low for fear of embarrassment for driving such a loud hunk of shit. Twenty or so people came running outside expecting to see a big, fast muscle car but instead, they got to see two drunken assholes in a Dodge Dynasty with no exhaust. Shaking their heads with disgust, they went back into the building while Jut and I parked.

"Well then... now that we've announced to the whole fucking U.P that we're here, let's go find some sluts!" Jut said as he took off the jacket which was wrapped around his head.

"Look, I know that it's embarrassing riding around in this thing but... c'mon man, really? Wrapping your head up to avoid being seen? You're such a dick." I said to Jut as we walked around the building into the back yard. Once we established our presence at the beer trailer out back and took up permanent standing positions right next to it, the fun started to begin.

We left the reception around Midnight which meant we stood there at the beer trailer for 3.5 hours straight. I'm not sure how much beer I personally drank but there were 9 kegs changed out while I was standing there. Seeing as though we were already pretty boozed up when we arrived, the sensation was now three fold intensified.

"C'mon Phillip! We're going to the bar!! Oh yeah, yer driving too! HAHAHA!" Jut said as he ran off with a gallon milk jug full of beer. We gathered up a couple other people, loaded up in the dynasty and sped off to town. Two of the girls in the back that we had acquired were shrieking in terror over the deafening roar of the Dynasty. They really lost it when I made a quick stop at some random guy's house to spin doughnuts in his yard with the throttle maxed out in reverse. I even managed to spare his nice apple tree that I almost hit by trying to run over a deer but got the birdbath instead. Beer cans and mud were flying through the air when I decided that we had best get the back on track.

We arrived at the down town scene approximately 1am. It took us a little longer to get to the bars as I was actually smart enough to leave my car on the outskirts of down town.

At the time it seemed like a smart idea but it failed to occur to me that the Dynasty could be heard up to 4 miles outside of town… five blocks wasn't going to do anything!

Damn near the whole wedding party was inside of the bar we went into. There was standing room only as we squeezed through to the waitress.

"What'll you have Sir?" She asked with a flirtatious wink of an eye.

"Jaeger bombs, ten of them!" I said as my fist

slammed down, full of $10 bills. "And after that round is gone, I want ten more of them!"

"YEAH!!" yelled Jut as he slapped a random woman's ass who was walking by. "Keep'em comin'!"

Tray after tray of Jaeger Bomb shots were consumed between me, Jut and every woman in our general area. I bought so many Jaeger bombs that they gave me a tray of ten for free. Hundreds of dollars later, the bar closed down at 2am. I remember paying the bar tab and I remember being horrified when I seen that it was well over 800 dollars... but I do not recall I how came to be outside the bar watching the Groom fight his best man. Jut and I were standing side by side cheering for the groom when another fight behind us broke out between the bride's mother and the some other woman.

"Ok, this is it man! This is our window!! Let's get

to the car and go!!" said Jut to me as he tugged on my coat. "Yeah." I said more to myself than anyone. "Let's do this." I held up my right hand to cover my right eye so I could minimize the amount of duplicates which my vision was producing and jogged to the car.

We were heading to the neighboring town to rendezvous with Jut's baby mama. Jut had the misfortune of taking her home one night after bar close and knocking her up. Almost a whole year later, he decided he wanted to make another with her so that's where we were heading. "What's in this for me Jut? I was promised sluts and the only thing I've got so far is drunk!" I yelled while driving with one hand down the interstate. "Drunk is an understatement. You backed into a telephone pole when we were leaving the parking lot!" Jut yelled back. "Well it shouldn't have been in my way!!"

I still had one eye covered up to minimize the effects of the double vision I had going on. In all honesty, I had no business behind that wheel but there we were, driving down the road at a rate of 45mph which sounded like 160mph. As we went roaring into a nice, quiet little suburb around 3am, multiple lights began to turn on in the surrounding houses. "Look! There it is!" Jut said excitedly, finishing his beer. "We're going to get laid for sure!!"

"Look Jut, I could care less about getting laid right now... I need.... I need a damn bed and a pillow." I begged as we walked towards the door"

"Shit! It's locked! Jut said with surprise"

"Does she even know you're coming?"

"Nope. I guess I'd better call her eh"

"No shit. I'm tellin ya Jut, I'm not driving around anymore tonight. I'll sleep in the back seat if I have to! These spins are *hic* getting out of control... *hic*"

As luck would have it, Jut's cell phone was lost at the bar somewhere and he didn't have her number memorized so we had to resort to plan B. Plan B consisted of Jut using a nonworking credit card to swipe between the door frame and the door itself. About 5 minutes into it, he managed to break into the house. Jut was leaning up against the door and I was leaning up against jut, trying to see what he was doing when the door suddenly opened. Jut fell first into the entry way followed with me falling on top of him. Landing on a big pile of boots and shoes, we both started laughing hysterically. As we threw shoes out of our way while trying to get up, we came face to face with the two, young teenage girl babysitters. They sat on the couch, huddled together with eyes that resembled a deer once it has been spotted in the headlights. The blanket which covered them was drawn up so all you could see was their nose up. Jut and I both froze in our tracks and stared at them for a good minute until he finally broke the awkward silence. "Look Phillip... Sluts! Let's fuck them!"

We immediately began laughing hysterically again which sent the babysitters into a fit of extreme horror. Once we were done laughing, Jut explained that he was one of the kid's fathers and that we were the good guys. After the explanation, we both ascended the stairs into the top floor's master bedroom. "Oh yeah, I forgot... she's still at work." Jut said as we both jumped on her king size bed.

The last thing I remember was Jut talking to her on the phone... he called her up at the local bar she worked at and promised that we would give her a ride home. It was raining sideways and thundering to beat hell outside and she didn't have her own vehicle. Upon hearing promises of a ride from work, the woman told her other driver that she had a ride.

The next thing I remember was waking up with some big girl who had a hand full of my hair. She was dripping wet and looked like she had just been through a war.

"Get the fuck out." She said in a firm tone of voice. She wasn't yelling but you could tell she was not very happy either. I stumbled my way down the hallway to the first room I seen with a bed and passed out in it.

I woke up to Jut standing above me, holding a baby in his arms and feeding it a bottle. Once my eyes opened, he said "C'mon Phillip, get your ass up. We gotta get the fuck out of here." He then proceeded to walk out of the room and back down the hallway. My head hurt so bad that it felt like someone beat me with a bat. I could literally smell the alcohol in the room and then I realized that the smell was coming from me. I looked down to notice that I was underneath a sponge bob sleeping bag and there were power ranger bed sheets covering the bed. As soon as started to sit up, a little boy from the bunk above looked down at me and asked: "Are you friends of my dad?"

"Who's your dad kid?" I asked in confusion.

"I don't know… that why I was hoping you could tell me!"

"Holy shit kid… it's way too early for this. Tell your damn mother to get her tubes tied." And with that, I staggered out into the hallway while rubbing my forehead with my palms. "Jut! Can we go?"

"Yep! Sorry baby but I gotta go… my friend is a recovering drug addict and we need to go get his meds." He said to the big lady who was lying half naked across the bed. We marched downstairs, put our shoes on and went into the Dynasty. Before I fired it up, I looked at him and said "A recovering drug addict? You're such a dick."

"Hey! Whatever works man! She understands... she's got very low morals and has had to deal with addicts in the past." said Jut as he started to wrap is head up in a hooded sweatshirt.

I just sat there and watched him for a couple minutes as he adjusted and fought with the hoodie.

"...you're a dick." was all I could say at that moment.

I fired up the Dynasty and revved it up as high as it would go for a good ten seconds straight. Black smoke was rolling out of the back as if the ole' girl were on fire. The sound echoed so loudly through the neighborhood that three kids just down the road fell off their bikes and one ran home crying.

"And you wonder why I wrap my face up!" Jut yelled as loud as he could.

"Still doesn't change the fact that you're a dick!!" I yelled back.

I reversed out of the driveway while giving it all the gas I could before slamming it into drive on the main road. The front tires squealed and created even more smoke which further scared the little kids. Jut reached into the back seat, grabbed us each a beer and then we started to make our way towards home.

Mission accomplished.

Legend of the immortal porcupine

My brother happened to be driving down the road on his way home from work one day when something out of the ordinary caught his attention. Near the top of a big elm tree that was on the side of the road sat one of the biggest porcupines he had ever seen. As luck would have it, my brother had his trusty .222 hornet with him and even had a couple extra shells to spend. He jumped out of his truck, loaded the rifle up and pumped 3 rounds into the porcupine. Instead of falling from the tree like usual, the porcupine got caught in the tree's crotch and stuck there. Feeling as though he had accomplished something rather important for the day, he resumed the drive home.

Later that same night, I was driving home from

the beer store when I came across the biggest porcupine I had ever seen! I pulled over, reached into the back and armed my .22 with a 30round clip and started spraying lead. Sticks, leaves and even a bird's nest fell from the tree as 30 bullets tore through them and the porcupine. Instead of falling from the tree though, the porcupine got wedged into a V shape in the tree and stayed there. "Well, all the better!" I thought. "Now everyone can see my prized trophy! Man, that's one hell of a big porcupine!" Proud of myself and the .22 for not jamming, I sped off to my brother's house to tell him about my big kill of the evening.

"You most certainly did not!" said my brother rather angrily "I shot that prick over 3 hours ago with my trusty hornet!"
"Really? I could have sworn I seen it moving

when I was shooting..." I said, disappointed that my brother laid claim to the porcupine.

"Yeah, when I shot it, it fell into that little crotch area and stuck there. You put thirty shells into'em and he didn't fall?"

"Nope... didn't even budge'em eh." I said, thinking back to the hailstorm of lead I threw at the porcupine.

As we sat there discussing the size of that porcupine, Billdo came running into my brother's house.

"Dude!! I just shot the biggest damn porcupine you ever did see!"

"Let me guess, it's stuck in the tree still?" I asked.

"How the hell did you know?" Billdo demanded

"I shot'em too about an hour ago." I replied

"And I shot'em about 2 hours before that!" Leo exclaimed proudly.

"Well shit guys! Way to ruin my damn story! And here I thought I was going to be famous for shooting such a big porcupine!" Billdo said in disgust. We all cracked open a beer and started discussing other matters which were not porcupine related. Little did we know though, that porcupine was going to be top topic of discussion by many people for months to come.

The next day, I went down to my Grandpa's farm to see what was going on and catch up on all the local gossip. The very first thing my Grandpa said to me was "So I shot a big porcupine this morning. The son of a bitch is still up in the tree too!" After I had explained that the brother, Billdo and I had already all taken turns shooting that same porcupine, the neighbor, Ed, came in and announced that he had just shot a huge porcupine. Almost at the same time, Grandpa and I asked: "Is it still up in the tree?"

"Hell yeah it's still in the tree! When I shot it, it fell into a Y and got stuck up there!"

"It didn't fall you damn liar! Grandpa said jokingly "It was already there because he's already dead! The grandson shot'em yesterday I guess... don't worry Ed, I shot at him this morning too... thought I had myself quite the prize" We all laughed, talked for a little while then went our separate ways as we all had stuff to do.

As I was driving down the road to work I saw someone pulled over on the road and standing outside of their vehicle. As I got closer to the vehicle and the person, I realized that they were armed and was shooting at the porcupine. They were so occupied with shooting at the already dead beast that they never noticed me until I was damn near on top of them.

"Phillip! Look what I just killed!" said Jut who was lobbing 20 gauge slugs at the dead beast.

"Dude... that thing has been dead for quite some time now... and damn near everyone has shot it!!"

"What do you mean?" Jut asked. I told'em how my brother was the original shooter and how others (including myself) had shot it as well.

"Well I'll be damned." Jut said while starting to chuckle. "I wonder how many shells have been put into it already?

"I'm not sure but I alone put in thirty rounds into it eh. I'm assuming that this porcupine is going to have a lot of lead launched at it... Ok man, I gotta get to work. Catch you later!" I yelled at Jut as I drove off down the road.

During my lunch hour, I went into the local restaurant to grab a bite to eat when I overheard two guys talking about the huge porcupine that was dead up in the tree outside of town. At least, they assumed it was dead because they never seen it move while they were looking at it. They were also going on about how horrible it is to shoot animals and how the shooter should have criminal charges against them and how they should call PETA ect…. I just laughed to myself and ate the rest of my lunch while I listened to them talk. It was apparent that these two gentlemen were greenies.

Greenies are the people who are against hunting, fishing and trapping. They also value the life of an animal's more than a humans and will riot if they see someone cut down a tree. Greenies and Yoopers mix like oil and water eh. Confirming that these two were nothing more than the previously mentioned when I seen their salads, I walked next to their table on my way out and said "You know the best thing about Greenies?"

Both men looked at me with confusion and asked "What's that?"

"It only takes 1 dead porcupine in a tree to get rid of'em all."

"....what?" the one man asked again, even more confused than before.

Unfortunately, his question fell on deaf ears as I was walking out of the restaurant with a big ole' grin on my face. Damn greenies anyway!

More than three weeks had gone by and the amount of people who had "shot the biggest porcupine ever" had grown exponentially. There were so many shooters now that I had lost count after the first week! Whenever you would drive by the porcupine now, you could note that the leaves and branches were cleared around it by at least 3 feet in all directions from all the bullets. There were also bullet holes all up and down the tree below and above the porcupine while the road was littered with spent shells. I stopped the one day with high hopes that someone dropped a golden plate on the side of the road as that's what it looked like from afar while driving. I was disappointed to find only a big pile of spent .223 shells though. There were even a couple of empty .338 rounds and a plethora of spent 10 gauge shells. "Holy shit," I thought "Yoopers don't fuck around when it comes to slow moving animals that are stuck in trees!"

Just as I was about to hop back into my truck, someone from behind me said "I wish you damn people would just leave that poor animal alone!" My damn heart nearly leapt forth from my chest as I had no idea anyone was there. Sure enough, two older (50s or so... freshly retired by the looks of things) people who had just moved into a house back in the woods were planting trees in their ditch.

"Excuse me?" I asked rather dumbfounded... this was the first time I had ever seen the new owners of the house.

"Every day for the last 3 weeks or so, at least four different people per day come and shoot at that damn porcupine! Is that all anyone does in this town? Throw beer cans out their window and shoot poor defenseless animals?" the gal asked me in a frank, disgusted tone.

"Well... uh... No. Not really. We fish quite often and shoot even bigger animals as well eh."

"Eh? What are you some kind of damn Canadian?" asked the man in a snobby tone of voice.

"No. Actually, I'm not. I'm a full blooded, home grown Yooper. Are you not?"

"No, we're not actually. We just moved here from Flint..."

"FLINT!?" I said, taken aback. "You're a troll!"

"Excuse me?"

"You heard me! You, Sir, are a troll and have no place up in these parts. I suggest you just let us Yoopers patrol these roads and shoot whatever we damn well please as this is no place for your kind." I told him with a figure pointed in his general direction.

"But the damn porcupine is dead and you damn whack jobs are STILL shooting at it!" he retorted angrily. "Even the gangs down in Flint don't shoot at each other this much!"

"Well, maybe you should go higher those gangs for protection then eh." I said as I stepped back and hopped back into my truck. "Trolls have no business in these parts. Mind your own damn business!" and with that, I drove off to spread the word that our nice quiet town had been infested with trolls.

About a week after the encounter with the newly relocated trolls, I ran into another friend of mine who had an "awesome story" to tell me. It involved pulling over on the side of the road and shooting the biggest porcupine he had ever seen in a tree and how it was still there.

"You should have seen it Phillip! It was running up the tree and I shot it dead as hell! He moved pretty quickly for a big guy!"

"Stop! Now I KNOW you're lying! That porcupine has been dead for over a month! I know for a fact that he wasn't running up that tree! My brother shot him originally and he's had about 400 rounds put through him ever since eh"

"Yeah… you're right… he wasn't running up the tree… it sure did look like he was moving though."

"Yeah, that poor bastard always looks like it's moving… maybe it's a sign from the Bullhead

Gods that we're doomed to keep wasting our ammo on that damn thing."

"Christ I hope you're wrong about that... don't the Bullhead Gods realize that the price of ammo is only getting more expensive?" asked my buddy.

"The Bullhead Gods do not care about prices... what they do care about is older, snobby trolls invading their lands... Wait a minute... that's it! Maybe the Bullhead Gods left that porcupine there to punish the trolls! Oh man, it's on now!" I said excitedly as I ran off to my truck.

"Where are you going?" asked my buddy in confusion.

"To do the God's bidding!"

Later that afternoon, a black Chrysler Fifth Avenue came rolling up ever so slowly in front of the tree which hosted the remains of the dead porcupine. An older couple who were planting even more trees in their ditch recognized the situation and could only stare at the car as if they were deer caught in its headlights. The car's tires screeched some from the sudden stop and all four doors opened at the same time. Five men with ski masks jumped out of the car, lined up on the side of the road and started firing at the porcupine relentlessly. We had a .308, .22, .300, .45 and an ak47 with a 30 round drum. It sounded like a street war had broken out for over a minute as four other friends and I stood there and shot round after round at the porcupine. After everyone had completely emptied their clips, we all piled back into the car and pulled up to the couple who were lying down in the ditch. "Not a fucking word about this to anyone!" Billdo yelled out the passenger side window. With that, we tried to spin the tires for a dramatic take off but failed miserably. The old bitch of a car just shot out a thick cloud of black smoke and stalled.

We all sat there with our ski masks still on as Jut kept trying to get the car started. After a good 15 seconds of turning it over, he revved the engine up as high as it would go and dumped it into drive. The tires didn't spin but we sure did leave a thick haze of black smoke in the air. Laughing like hell and high fiving each other for a good job of scaring the trolls, we went straight to the beer store to celebrate.

The next week at work, one of my buddies came into the office and told me about a "huge porcupine" that he had shot just off the road in a tree. I laughed at him and then explained the tale of the immortal porcupine and how my brother was the original shooter. After we had a few more laughs, he happened to mention a nice chunk of land that had come up for sale by owner... Forty acres of land with a house back in the forest which happens to be located directly across the road from where the porcupine is hanging.

All hail the Bullhead Gods!

The Misadventures of Uncle Dave - I

So I woke up one morning to find that I had a really bad cold. I was around the age of 7, was still in school and my parents worked full time so I had to go to a babysitter's house. On this particular day, the only one my mother could find to watch me was my Grandma so I was hauled down to the farm for some rest and a day off of school to recover. After a couple hours of lying in bed, sipping on homemade chicken soup and chewing on cough drops, my Uncle Dave entered the house.

Uncle Dave was about 5'10, 170lbs and had a reddish colored beard that took up a majority of his face. He had an IQ that rivaled genius status but was usually too boozed up to utilize it properly. His voice was so loud that it could carry for hundreds of yards in all directions by simply talking. He also had a cackling laugh that sounded like some kind of sick animal which could be heard anywhere within a mile. Yeah, Uncle Dave was a hell of a good guy but could be very, very intimidating to little kids and at this time, I was still just a little kid.

The door to the bedroom I was in flew open as if someone had kicked it down and there stood my Uncle Dave holding a Budweiser in his hand. Seeing as though it was only 9:00AM, I was rather surprised to see him holding a beer this early in the morning.

"What the hell is wrong with you kid? What are you some kind of a pussy?" Uncle Dave asked through clenched teeth while giving me a soul penetrating glare.

"No… I'm sick so I had to stay home from school…"

"Bullshit! You're just faking so you can lay around all day! Well, that's not gunna happen kid! Do you hear me? It's NOT gunna happen!!" He dragged me out of bed and through my pair of shoes at me. "Put'em on! We're going sailing!" Uncle Dave said while grabbing a case of Budweiser from the fridge.

"Oh no you don't David!" yelled my Grandma who was shaking her fist at my Uncle. "He's sick and needs his rest!"

"He's not sick. He's just faking it so he didn't hafta go to school. I used to do it all the time Ma! We're going sailing and spending the day in the sun. We'll be back later!"

As we walked out the door, I could still hear my grandma yelling at Uncle Dave not to take me but it didn't seem to slow him down. He tossed the case of beer on the seat of his Ford F-150 right between us and away we went.

Thirty minutes later we were boarding his sailboat which was named the "Sea Wolf" and he was barking out orders like I was a seasoned sailor. "Grab that rope! Lower the keel! Hook up the tiller! Grab me a beer! Grab one for yourself! Raise the main!"

"Uncle Dave, I don't know what you are talking about" I told him as I grabbed us a beer. "I've never been sailing before…"

"Never been sailing!? What the hell is wrong with you!?" he asked by yelling directly in my face. "Well then, let me learn you a thing or two!" After about forty minutes of learning the names of everything, how to operate the ropes and tie them correctly, Uncle Dave figured it was time to shove off.

As we got under way down the river with the main sail hoisted and catching some good wind,

Uncle Dave began to explain to me how the boom worked.

"Ok, this goddamn river is only so wide so we're going to have to zigzag our way down it. You see that water buoy? Once we get close to it, you're going to have to turn to the port side and take us back to the other side of the river. Once we hit that side, we turn back this way. Do you understand boy?" he asked as he took a long drink from his beer and lit up a Camel cigarette.

"Yeah, I understand Uncle Dave." I said as I fought with the tiller to keep us in a straight line.

"So once we get up here a little bit and turn, the boom here is going to swing to the other side really, really fast. When it does, you need to duck or it'll take your fucking head clean off your shoulders!"

"Ok Uncle, I think I got it."

"You think!? You're a man! You don't think! You

KNOW!" he yelled directly into my face again. At this time, I was very nervous. I was fully in charge of steering the sail boat and had zero desire to let my Uncle Dave down by messing something up.

"Ok, start turning!" he barked as I began to turn us the other direction. "Now remember what I said earlier… we're going to start turning and…" he was suddenly cut off when the wind caught the main sail just right and sent the boom swinging violently to the other side of the boat. Uncle Dave was standing up, talking to me while holding a Budweiser in one hand and a cigarette in the other. The boom hit him so hard in the back of the head that his cigarette went flying into my face and melted some of my eye brow. His beer went flying over the side of the boat and he damn near went with it. The only reason he didn't get thrown overboard was because his cut off jean shorts managed to get snagged on one of the rope tie offs, stopping him just short of falling over the side.

"You see!? You see that shit!?" he yelled as he struggled to get himself upright again. "That's what happens when you don't duck! You get slapped in the back of your fucking head and lose your beer!"

A few hours into the voyage, I had the boat and its ways down pretty good. Uncle Dave was pretty drunk at this point but I only had the one beer. He insisted that I keep drinking because "that's what men do" but I was only 7 and didn't much care for the taste of Budweiser. As we were holding a nice line across the river, Uncle Dave launched into a story about when he was in the Military. He was stationed in the Philippines as Military Police and often grew bored with patrolling the two miles of road they had in the particular town he was in. When given enough time, anyone can find something to do that will surely entertain their self.

"...so I was driving down the only two damn miles of road the shithole town had the one day and I decided to stop at the dump, you know. I got out of the truck and seen an Iguana!
Do you know what an Iguana is? It's a BIG FUCKING LIZZARD! FUCKING BIG!" he said as his arms spread out as wide as they would go.
At this point, Uncle Dave was wearing nothing but his frayed up cut off jean shorts and yelling as loud as he could. He was standing at the bow of the boat with his wild hair blowing in the breeze, likening him to a drunken pirate. He once again had a can of Budweiser in one hand and a lit camel cigarette in the other. Beer and ashes

were flying into the breeze and he continued on, yelling out his story.

"So I'd take out my standard issued 9mm Beretta and go 'BLAM BLAM BLAM' at this big fucking lizard, you know! I'd shoot at those cock suckers until I was completely out of ammo! So once I was out of ammo, I'd go see the munitions officer and ask for some more! He would ask; 'what did you do with your other ammo?'
And I would say; 'I shot it all off!'
He would say back; 'At what?'
I would tell him; 'Iguanas!! You know what those are, don't you!? They're these BIG FUCKING LIZZARDS!!!!'"

Uncle Dave was really getting into the spirit of the story at this time. Jumping up and down with his empty can of beer held in his hands to act as an imaginary 9mm pistol, he kept yelling his story to his 7yr old nephew.

"So after I got my ass chewed for shooting all those goddamn iguanas, you'll never guess what happened! That's right! HE GAVE ME MORE AMMO!!!! HAHAHAH!!!!!!! SO WHAT DID I DO!??! I WENT BACK AND SHOT MORE FUCKING IGUANAS!!! BLAM BLAM BLAM BLAM!!! HAHAHAHAHAHA!"

While he was laughing hysterically and trying not to fall off the boat from being so drunk, I was still sitting at the tiller holding an empty beer can (to fake out Uncle Dave so he would stop trying to feed me beer) and getting kind of scared. We were getting close to where he kept the sail boat and I had no idea how to dock it. "Hey Uncle Dave, can you take over and dock this thing? My arms are getting sore." I told him as I pretended to drink more beer out of the empty can. "Pussy!" he snorted. With as much grace as a three legged horse, he began to make his way to the back of the boat. Half way across he somehow managed to get tangled in a stray rope that was lying across the hull and under the boom. "What the... what the fuck!" he yelled with displeasure. "Who put this death trap here like this!! This is how people fucking die!" he bent over and was getting his legs untied while I began to make the final turn back towards the dock. Just as the boom started to swing from port side to starboard, Uncle Dave stood up just in time to catch it with the side of his head. There was a camel cigarette hanging out of his mouth and when the boom made contact, it sent a shower of sparks flying into the air.

Imagine driving down the road at 60mph and

throwing a lit cigarette out of the window. You know that shower of sparks that explodes when it first makes contact with the asphalt? The boom had the same exact effect when it slapped Uncle Dave in the head.

This time he just fell flat on his stomach and didn't even move. I was sure that he was dead and immediately started to think about how I was going to explain this to my parents...
"Yeah... Uncle Dave kidnapped me from Grandmas, took me sailing, taught me about lizards and how to drink beer... then I accidently killed him with the boom..." Just as I was about to yell his name he began to move around some. He rolled over onto his back and laid there for a few seconds before sitting up. "You see, that's why you gotta duck when you turn." He said rather calmly.

"I did."

"Well that's good because I sure fucking didn't!"

"Hey Uncle Dave?"

"What kid?"

"You're on fire." I said and lifted a finger to point at his head. His long reddish beard hair was smoldering from the cigarette sparks and he began to slap himself in the face, trying to put it out. "I'M ON FIRE!" he yelled as he continued to slap himself. After thirty seconds or so of jumping around and yelling, he managed to extinguish his beard and sit back down. "Holy shit... I need a beer!"

"Do you really think you need another one Uncle Dave?"

"Boy, I've puked more beer in my life than you've ever drank!"

"Uncle Dave... I'm seven."

"Excuses are like assholes! Everyone's got one!"

he yelled then started cackling hysterically. "Get out of the way and let me show you how to dock!" he shoved me out of the way, nearly knocking me out of the boat and grabbed the tiller. I sat with my back towards the bow of the boat and against the cabin hull so I could have something to lean on while keeping a good eye on Uncle Dave. "Ok, we'll go a little bit further then we'll drop the main sail and coast in on the trolling motor." We were skipping along the water at a fairly good pace and Uncle Dave began explaining how to start taking down the sail when we struck something. He was standing upright with one hand barely on the tiller and the other with a can of Budweiser pointing at the sail when the keel on the bottom of the boat struck ground. The impact was a hard one and it sent Uncle Dave flying head first through the plastic door of the cabin quarters without giving him the chance to react. I was perfectly fine as my back was placed firmly against the hull, next to the door. I watched wide eyed as my Uncle busted the door with his head. "Uncle Dave! Are you ok?" I yelled into the cabin. "So, the lesson here is, you always need to raise the keel when you start getting into shallow water." he said through a pile of beer cans and empty cigarette boxes. I reached in to give him a hand but he just slapped it away as he straightened himself out. "If you really want to help me, grab me another beer! Mine spilled again!"

"I can't Uncle Dave."

"Why the hell not?" he demanded.

"We're out. The last beer you had fell overboard and sank." I said while not knowing what to expect next. "Well, at least we're close to the dock now… You work on raising that keel and I'll pull down the sail." Once the both tasks were complete, we trolled into the dock and parked the boat in its usual spot. We tied the boat up and began to walk to his truck when I noticed what time it was on a clock which was on the side of a building. "Uncle Dave! It's 4:40pm! I've got to get home! Mom and Dad are already both home from work! I'm supposed to be sick and in bed today!" I said, my voice tainted with worry. "Bah. They know you're with me. You'll be fine! Now, how about a burger and some fries? My treat!" With those magic words from Uncle Dave, my worries about getting in trouble vanished. "Besides, it's a good place for me to get some more beer!" We hopped in his truck and began to pull out of the parking lot. Without any thought to fact that he had already consumed a case of beer and was now driving, I began to laugh as we side swiped someone's white car on our way out.

The Misadventures of Uncle Dave- II

"I'll take a Budweiser and the kid here will take a burger basket with fries." Uncle Dave said to the waitress as we pulled up a seat to the bar.

"Would you like something to drink cutie?" She asked me.

"Can I just have some water ma'am?"

"WATER!?" Uncle Dave yelled at me. "You don't drink water kid! Fish fuck in it! Get'em a coke instead, eh beautiful." The waitress just stood there with her mouth agape, staring at Uncle Dave and I. It seemed like she wanted to laugh (or call child protection services) but she kept a professional demeanor and went into the back with our orders.

A few minutes later I was finishing up my burger and Uncle Dave was four beers deep into a serious conversation with a native guy who was on the other side of him.

"I don't give a shit who you are, Indians just didn't have the conventional weaponry to fight back properly against the might of the U.S. military! I mean, think about it! You and I get into a fight right now and we each get to choose one weapon. Which would you pick? A good pistol or a fucking bow and arrow?" Uncle Dave yelled at the native.

"...bows and arrows worked well enough against General Custer" the Native replied.

"That may be, but it they didn't work good enough to keep you guys from living on reservations did they!?" Uncle Dave spat and began to laugh hysterically.

"Hey Kid!" he yelled directly into my face.

"Squanto here says bows and arrows are the best thing in the world!"

"I said no such thing Dave" said the Native man

on the other side of Uncle Dave.

"YOU DID TOO!" he yelled and slammed his fist on the bar.

"Bar wench! Get the bar a round and grab my nephew here another coke!" Uncle Dave was all sorts of wound up and drunk at this point. He eyes were glazed over and he smelled like a brewery. His speech was beginning slur and he was practically yelling at people who were sitting right next to him, including me.

"Casinos! Lots of'em! We need to make Casinos kid! Be like the Indian here and take everyone's money so we can live at the bar!" upon making this statement, he began to stare at the wall full of whiskey bottles used to poor shots. He sat there quietly while looking at the wall and it was then that I noticed he wasn't even looking at it... he was staring *through* the wall, as if he was reliving a fond memory or thinking really hard.

He sat like this for a good minute before he took another drank of his beer and said in a low, thoughtful tone: "live at the bar..."

After everyone got their free drink from Uncle Dave and he managed to finish off three more beers in the matter of minutes, he announced that it was time for us to leave. "Holy shit kid! It's damn near 8 o'clock! We gotta get you home before your mother flips out!" He threw a wad full of twenties on the bar (without counting) then grabbed me by the arm and yanked me out of my bar stool. The coke I was sipping on dumped all over the bar but it didn't stop him from rushing us outside. I asked him on the way out: "Should we clean up the coke I just spilled Uncle Dave?"

"Clean up after yourself at the bar? HAH! That's like telling a prostitute that she has to pay YOU after you tear her asshole!"

"What?"

"Tear her asshole! Telling her to pay you! You know?"

"No, not really… what's a prostitute? I asked completely dumbfounded.

"C'mon kid, you're busting my balls here. Let's just get in the truck and go eh." He said back to me as we approached the truck. Once we hopped in, he sat there for at least forty seconds trying to put the key into the ignition when he finally realized that there was already a key in it. "Holy shit kid, maybe I shouldn't be driving after all eh." he said loudly then started cackling. "Do you wanna drive?"

"Uncle Dave, I'm only seven and I've never driven a truck before…"

"Well what good are ya then!?" he yelled as he turned on the truck. He put it into gear and pressed the gas but we didn't go anywhere. We just sat in the same spot while the engine revved up higher and higher. "It's fucking busted!" He said angrily as he kept revving up the engine. "Oh wait, no it isn't… we're just in neutral is all." We pulled out of the parking lot and made it a few miles down the road before anyone said anything. "So, did you have fun today kid?" he asked with a smile, looking at me.

"I sure did Uncle Dave! I learned all sorts of stuff about sailing!" I replied.

"Including what not to do?" he asked with an eyebrow raised.

"Especially what not to do!" He started laughing then, in mid chuckle, started yelling and screaming with rage. "COCK SUCKER!!!" he yelled as we violently swerved across the road. "ROTTEN BASTARD!" he yelled again as he threw is 'road beer' at me and gripped the wheel with both hands just in time to safely pilot us into the ditch. We were only going about 50mph and the ditch we went into was completely dry and full of weeds. We had a soft landing and we both had on our seatbelts but I was highly confused as to what exactly just happened. We were sitting in the ditch with the truck still idling and Uncle Dave was still cussing up a storm. I noticed that his left arm (which he had hanging out the window) was bleeding and I couldn't help but asked what happened. "Must have been a bee or something... it hit my arm and damn ripped it off!" He stuck his arm towards me and I noticed the cut in his arm which was about an inch long. He suddenly started to rip the sleeveless shirt he was wearing into shreds and began to tie up the wound. "Like that? That's how we bandaged shit up back in the service kid. You can also use your socks as shit paper too, remember that." He said sincerely as he finished tying off his arm.

We backed out of the ditch without any problems and began to make our way back home again. By the time I got home, my mother was about ready to call the cops and file a missing person report. "Where have you been Dave!?" she yelled at her brother. "He is sick and was supposed to be at the farm resting!" Uncle Dave was still sitting in the truck with a full can of beer resting on the dash board and a tattered, torn up shirt barely covering his chest when he said; "He's not sick, he's just faking! He was fine while we were at the bar eh."

"The WHAT!?" my mother yelled, demanding an explanation that she would never get. As soon as I hopped out of the truck, Uncle Dave spun out in reverse and sent gravel flying all over her. Once he hit the paved road, he threw an empty beer can out of the window for good measure and sped off down the road. Mom just stood there, horrified. She stared at me for a good minute before saying "C'mon, let's go get you ready for bed and give you some medicine. We were almost to the front door when Uncle Dave's truck come hauling ass down the road and pulled back into the driveway. "Here! The little bastard's gunna need this!" He threw my school backpack out the window and into the driveway before he peeled out of the drive way again without saying bye. I ran over to my backpack, picked it up and ran back to my mother who was standing at the front door shaking her head with displeasure. As I walked into the porch, I opened my backpack and watched a dozen mostly-empty beer cans and a couple empty packs of camels fall out onto the ground. I looked up at my mother with wide eyes full of fear. Without saying a word, she cleaned up the mess, grabbed my backpack and threw it into the garbage. "Uncle Dave will buy you another one tomorrow." She said in fact.

"Do I have to go with him to get it?" I asked with worry

"NO!" she said with her eyes wide in horror. After a couple seconds of thinking, she asked me "So, what did you guys do today anyways?"

"…uhm… we went sailing…"

"And then?"

"We went to the bar and decided that we're going to build casinos."

Mom shook her head with disgust and told me that she didn't want to hear or know anymore. That night after I got showered up and ready for bed, Mom came in my room and made me recite all the prayers I knew twice over "just because".

Made in the USA
Charleston, SC
03 December 2012